YOU ARE ABOUT TO SET OFF
ON AN ADVENTURE WITH

INDIANA JONES ™

As this book opens, you and Indy will begin a secret voyage to Malekula, a mysterious island in the Coral Sea.

Why is Malekula called Horror Island? What strange curse does it carry? And what dark secrets are buried in its tangled jungles?

You will learn the answers to these questions as you and Indy challenge the curse of Malekula. You will choose your own actions and decide your own fate by following the directions at the bottom of each page.

If you make the right choices, your many adventures in this book will be exciting—and successful.

If you make the wrong choices, you and Indy may be trapped on Horror Island *forever*!

HAPPY TRAVELS!

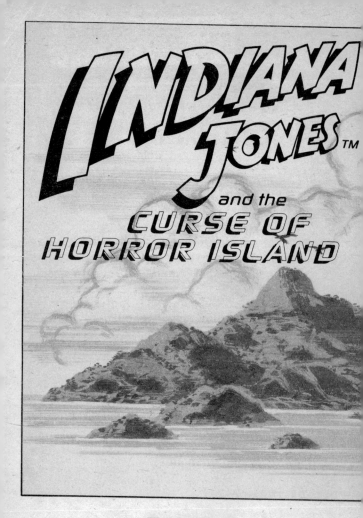

INDIANA JONES™
and the
CURSE OF
HORROR ISLAND

by *R. L. STINE*
Illustrated by DAVID B. MATTINGLY

BALLANTINE BOOKS • NEW YORK

RLI: $\dfrac{\text{VL: } 5+\text{up}}{\text{IL: } 5+\text{up}}$

Library of Congress Catalog Card Number: 84-90851

ISBN 0-345-31665-7

Designed by Gene Siegel

Cover and interior art by David B. Mattingly

Manufactured in the United States of America

First Edition: June 1984

INDIANA JONES™
and the
CURSE OF HORROR ISLAND

Find Your Fate™ Adventure #1

"Hey, you—watch out!"

You jump out of the way as a cart piled high with steamer trunks rumbles past you. A gigantic ocean liner has just pulled into port, and passengers are streaming down the gangplank, filling the pier with noise and confusion.

This has been the most exciting summer of your life—and it's only June! You had no idea when school let out that your parents were sending you to spend the summer with your cousin Indiana Jones. And you had no idea that as soon as you arrived, Cousin Indy would get a mysterious assignment—an assignment that would take both of you to a small jungle island in the South Pacific!

"This is better than going to summer camp!" you shout over the noise of the crowded pier.

"Take it easy, kid," Indy says, pushing his battered hat back on his head. "Look for Pier 66."

Craaack!

What was that sound?

Craaack. Craack!

Gunfire! Somebody is shooting at you!

....
Turn to page 2.

"Somebody doesn't want us to set sail," Indy says as the two of you duck behind a stack of luggage. His eyes narrow as he scans the pier.

Pinnnng!

A bullet bounces off the suitcase in front of you.

"I think there's more than one of them," Indy says. "We're sitting ducks here. We've gotta move out."

"Look—there's Pier 66 right ahead!" you cry, pointing. "That must be our boat." You see a small red cargo boat bobbing up and down in the dark water.

"If we try to make a run for the boat, we'll be easy targets," Indy says. "Maybe we should run into the crowd and try to lose them in the confusion."

Which way should you run?

If you decide to try for the cargo boat, turn to page 8.

If you decide to run into the crowd, turn to page 19.

"Hit the dirt!" Indy screams. "Lie perfectly still."

You do just as he says.

The flapping wings grow nearer, nearer. The chamber fills with a high-pitched squeal.

The killer bats are right overhead now. They fly over you, out the entrance to the excavation, out into the night, where they encounter the mercenaries who are pursuing you.

"AAAAAAIIIIIIEEEEEEE!"

You hear the cries of horror as the killer bats attack the mercenaries. The cries of horror quickly become cries of pain.

"Nasty little beasts, aren't they?" Indy says, climbing to his feet and pulling you up. "Let's not wait around for them to return. If I remember the map right, there should be a nice quiet chamber just beyond this tunnel where we can spend the night."

Exhausted, you follow Indy into the chamber. You lie down on the dirt floor and are asleep in seconds.

What will morning bring?

. . . .

Turn to page 4.

Sunlight trickles down into the underground chamber as morning comes. You pull yourself to your feet, feeling stiff and not very rested.

"How about some scrambled eggs and sausages?" Indy asks.

"Sounds good to me," you say, your eyes opening wide in anticipation.

"Sounds good to me too," Indy says. "We'll have to eat some when we get back to the States!"

The two of you spend the morning searching through the tunnels and caverns of the excavation, searching for the dove's hiding place.

At last Indy thinks he has found it. He pulls a rock out of the side of an excavation wall and reaches into the hole. "A bird in the hand is worth two in the...museum!" he cries, pulling out the ebony dove.

As he holds up the ancient sculpture to show it to you, the eerie cries that you heard the night before grow louder.

Is the dove really cursed? Is that an evil spirit crying out to you?

Turn to page 12.

Indy pulls out his pistol, aims carefully, and fires. The little gun goes *ping*! How can Indy bring down such huge beasts with that little pistol?

But the pistol works. The lead boar drops to its knees, raises its ugly head, and utters a final cry of agony.

Ping.

A second wild boar falls. Then a third.

The boars slow down. They seem confused. Some run off to the right, some to the left. Maybe—just maybe—Indy's plan is working!

Yes! The boars turn. They are running away from the clearing. Suddenly you hear human cries at the other side of the clearing.

The Malekulan natives have found you—and they are now directly in the path of the stampeding boars!

You close your eyes. You cannot keep their screams from your ears, but at least you can shut out the sight of their hideous deaths.

"Well, maybe we can make our way to the excavation in peace and quiet now," Indy says.

....

But he doesn't know what awaits you on page 13.

5

You leap up at the man and push the gun out of his hand. With a menacing hiss, Indy's whip wraps around him. Startled, the man cries out for help, but there is no one to come to his aid.

"Good work, kid!" Indy cries. "We got this guy all gift-wrapped. Who should we give him to?"

"Wait, Indy—look!" you cry, pointing to the pier. "The cargo boat—it's about to leave!"

"Uh-oh. Sorry we don't have time to wish you a formal bon voyage," Indy says. He pulls the bullwhip away, spinning the man off the pier and into the water below. "Let's catch that boat!" Indy cries to you, starting to run toward Pier 66. "If we miss it, it's a long swim to where we're going!"

Where are you headed?

Turn to page 16 to find out.

Indy reaches for his pistol, but the panther is on him too quickly. The gun flies out of Indy's hand as the panther leaps onto his chest, pushing him down to the ground.

Indy wrestles on the ground with the snarling creature as you watch helplessly. Now Indy is on top of the panther. Captain Jim raises his pistol to shoot Indy. You kick the pistol out of his hand.

Indy grabs the front and back legs of the struggling animal and lifts it up into the air. With a mighty heave, he tosses the surprised cat onto the blond man.

The panther, furious now, lashes out at its master. In seconds the blond man lies dead on the ground. The panther runs off into the jungle.

Meanwhile, you have handed Captain Jim's gun to Indy, who now has it trained on Captain Jim. "Wrestling isn't really my sport," Indy says, wiping at the long panther scratches on his neck, "but I guess I won that match."

He picks up the ebony dove from the ground and examines it. "Wait a minute!" he cries. "This dove is a fake!"

Turn to page 28.

"Keep your head down, kid, and don't run in a straight line!" Indy yells. "Just run *fast*!"

You both leave the safety of the luggage pile and run toward Pier 66 and the cargo boat.

Bullets whistle over your head. There are screams and the loud footsteps of people rushing to get out of your way and away from the gunfire. But all you see is the red cargo boat waiting at the other end of the dock.

Then you hear an angry voice. "Freeze or I'll shoot!" A policeman is standing at the edge of the pier, his pistol drawn. "Don't take another step!"

"Keep running, kid!" Indy yells. "Get to the boat!"

"But the policeman can help us!" you yell. What should you do?

....

Run right past the policeman to get to the boat? If that's your choice, turn to page 27.

Stop and ask the policeman for help? If that's your choice, turn to page 35.

9

Your voyage to Malekula is short and uneventful. You go ashore and head into the steamy jungle. Indy follows his map to the low hills where Professor Ravenwood made his excavations years earlier.

"Hey, what's going on here?" Indy cries. You look at the excavation site. It is surrounded by a barbed-wire fence. "The Malekulans wouldn't use barbed wire! Who in blazes has done this?" Indy cries.

Then you see two armed men patrolling the fence. You climb a low hill to the east of the excavation and find a tunnel opening that hasn't been fenced off. "In here—quick!" Indy whispers.

The tunnel winds its way into the main chamber of the excavation. You peer out into the lighted chamber from the darkness of the tunnel. You see dozens of men unloading the contents of hundreds of wooden crates.

"Smugglers!" Indy whispers. "They must be stealing these crates off the docks at New Guinea and storing them here. I'll bet they started the rumors about a curse on this island to keep people away!"

You both duck down as an armed guard walks by just a few yards in front of you. "They must have taken the dove out of here a long time ago," Indy whispers. "Let's go, kid."

You turn to go back into the tunnel. Then a voice calls, "Stop where you are! You two aren't going anywhere!"

....

Turn to page 29.

Indy grabs the bullwhip coiled around his shoulder and pulls it free, ready to attack this intruder.

"Your whip is of little use against *this*!" the man cries, stepping out of the shadows to reveal a pistol in his hand.

Indy's jaw drops in astonishment as he recognizes the man with the gun. "Professor Huntington!" he cries.

"I'm sorry you remembered me, Jones," Huntington says with a scowl. "Now I'll have to kill you—and your friend there!"

"You—you were with the original expedition," Indy says, taking a few steps toward the professor, still grasping the handle of his bullwhip. "Have you come to try to take the dove for yourself?"

"I don't have to *try*—I *have* it!" Huntington cries. He picks up the treasure chest and starts to run out of the chamber.

Indy sees his chance and rushes forward to attack with his bullwhip.

"Wait!" you cry. "Let him go! There's no need to fight him!"

Indy stops and looks at you in surprise. He can't decide whether to listen to you or not.

....

Should Indy attack Huntington to keep him from leaving with the treasure chest? If so, turn to page 24.

Should he wait, as you've suggested? If so, turn to page 32.

11

The frightening cries, like some kind of ghostly crowing, echo off the dirt walls of the excavation chamber. "Let's get out of here!" you say.

"Where's your sense of adventure, kid?" Indy asks. "We have to find out what's making that awful racket!"

Sense of adventure? You've had enough adventure to last you the rest of your life! But Indy insists on following the sound.

You walk through a long tunnel. The cries become louder and louder. You enter a vast chamber—and you see what is making these eerie sounds.

Chickens.

Chickens and roosters.

Indy tosses his hat in the air and laughs, the only time you've ever seen him laugh. "This is the ancient curse!" he cries. "These are the evil spirits! Chickens!"

"Okay, can we go now?" you ask impatiently.

"We have one problem, kid," says Indy. "The natives of this place are going to be waiting outside for us. And as you recall, they're not too friendly. How are we going to get us—and this black bird—past them?"

Turn to page 30.

You walk along the narrow jungle path until you come to an area of low hills. "Look—an opening!" you cry, pointing toward the tallest hill. "That must be the excavation."

"You win the prize, kid," says Indy. "Let's climb up and take a look."

As you start up the hill you hear a frightening sound, halfway between a roar and a shriek. You look up to see a large, furry beast at the entrance to the excavation. Suddenly it sees you, throws back its head, and shrieks again.

"Holy moly!" mutters Indy. "Maybe the creatures on this island really are cursed!"

Just then you see a tunnel cut into the hill. "Let's duck in here, kid," says Indy. "Maybe we can avoid our friend up there."

You climb into the tunnel. As your eyes begin to adjust to the dark, you hear a soft rustling sound right next to you. Then you see it. A huge scorpion—and it's heading straight for you!

Turn to page 64.

You and Indy practically dive down the stairs to the lower deck. You stumble through the darkness until you find a large supply locker. You pull open the door and climb inside, pulling the door shut behind you.

Footsteps echo on the deck above you, and then you hear them on the stairway to the lower deck.

The footsteps stop.

Silence.

"There's no one here, Brady," says a man's voice. "Let's get goin'. We got those three mugs for questioning. That's a good night's work."

"That's fine with me, Sergeant," you hear Brady reply.

A few minutes later the boat is silent again. You and Indy are alone.

Or are you?

As you open the supply locker you hear a muffled cry coming from the cargo hold.

"We seem to be sharing our accommodations," Indy says, drawing his pistol. "Let's go introduce ourselves!"

Go on to page 15.

You push open the steel locker door and burst into the cargo hold. There on the floor, bound and gagged, are the boat's captain and crew.

"Boy, someone sure doesn't want you to get where you're going, Indiana," the captain says after you have untied him and his men. "I say we get out of port—right away!"

"That's fine with us!" Indiana says, grinning. "This trip has *got* to get better!"

A short while later you are steaming out into the ocean. The night stars are reflected in the dark waves beneath you. It is the most beautiful sight you have ever seen.

Your destination is the tiny jungle island of Malekula, located just southeast of New Guinea in the Coral Sea. In 1933 this is a slow voyage of many weeks—especially on a cargo boat as small as yours.

Why are you headed for this distant island?

Turn to page 43.

A few moments later you are aboard the cargo boat and it is sailing out to sea. It isn't until that evening after dinner that Indy decides to tell you where you are headed.

"We're going to a place known as Horror Island," he begins.

"I think I'll take Hawaii instead."

"It wasn't always called Horror Island," Indy continues, ignoring your remark. "It was only called that after the people there came to believe the island was cursed."

"Oh, this is starting to sound better and better!"

"Listen, kid, it wasn't my idea that you tag along," Indy replies, leaning against the rail and staring out to sea. "If your parents knew I'd brought you, they'd have my neck!"

16

The small boat lurches forward in the water, throwing you against the rail. "I'm sorry," you say. "I'm having a great time. Really." You pick yourself up off the deck.

"Well..." Indy continues his explanation, "the real name of this island we're going to is Malekula. The man who taught me just about everything I know about archeology, Professor Abner Ravenwood, led an expedition there a few years ago."

"And what did he find?"

"Trouble," answers Indy.

Turn to page 18.

"Professor Ravenwood went to Malekula in hopes of finding the remains of an ancient civilization buried in the jungle. But he failed. Or, I should say, he wasn't given a chance to succeed."

"I don't understand," you say. "Who stopped him?"

"The Malekulans. In his digging he disturbed some ancient burial ground. The natives believed that he had freed evil spirits and brought a curse upon the island. So they chased Professor Ravenwood away. As a matter of fact, he was lucky to escape with his life. That was the only lucky part to the expedition."

"Why are we going back?" you ask. "To find the evil spirits?"

"Nope," says Indy, staring at the churning waters. "Just after you arrived on campus, I got a call from Marcus Brody, the curator of the National Museum. He found some of Professor Ravenwood's papers and a map. The papers referred to a carving, an ebony dove that Ravenwood had dug up on Malekula. The dove is an ancient idol, sculpted on the island more than two thousand years ago. We think it's still there. My job is to get it for the National Museum. The trouble we had back in port means that there are others who'd like to get the dove too. This could be tricky!"

Turn to page 80.

You both leap away from the luggage pile. Another bullet whizzes over your heads. You slip into the line of passengers who have just disembarked, and Indy turns to see if you are still being followed.

Two men in trenchcoats are just a few yards behind you. Their hands are in their trenchcoat pockets, but you can see that they are carrying guns. Their eyes survey the crowd. They spot you!

You dart through the crowd of people, cutting back in the direction of the cargo ship.

"This isn't working, kid," Indy says, seeing that you still haven't lost your pursuers. "We've gotta try something else."

There's a stack of large wooden crates on the pier in front of the red cargo boat. "Maybe we could hide in those crates," you suggest.

"Worth a try," Indy says. "The crates will be loaded onto the boat, and we'll be home free. Let's go!"

You run to the crates. Indy pries open the one at the far end of the pier and pushes you inside, quickly closing the lid. From inside the dark crate, you hear him climbing into another crate.

Now you wait to be lifted onto the cargo boat.

Have you managed to escape the men in the trenchcoats?

....

Turn to page 103.

You follow a narrow path through the tangled trees. The path soon becomes covered with overgrown vines and tree roots, and you have to cut your way through with machetes.

After an hour Indy looks up at the sky through the thick, leafy trees. "Wait a minute, Captain!" he cries. "I think we're going in the wrong direction."

Captain Jim wheels around angrily and pushes his good eye right up to Indy's face. "Don't tell me which way to go, you young pup. I remember this jungle as well as I remember my left eye!"

"Okay, okay," Indy says, backing away. "You lead—we'll follow."

You continue to cut your way through the jungle until you come to a clearing. In the clearing stand three tents. "What's going on here?" Indy asks. "Whose camp is this?"

"Welcome, Jones," calls a familiar voice. The man with the wavy blond hair, the man who tried to block your way back in the port in New York, steps out from one of the tents. Holding a pistol on the two of you, he gives Captain Jim a little wave. "Thank you, Jim," he says. "You did your job well. You've delivered the goods!"

"Now," says the man, grinning, "would you like to see the ebony dove before you die?"

Turn to page 34.

20

"You there!" the man's voice cries. "Stop!"

Indy draws his pistol. He raises it and tries to aim in the dark.

Zinnnnng!

Indy's pistol flies out of his hand.

The man has shot first. He is obviously not a friend.

Who is he—and what does he want?

Turn to page 76.

It is the last cry Huntington will ever make.

The rats are upon him. You turn away. You cannot bear to watch their merciless attack.

Indy grabs his bullwhip and cracks it in the air. The noise startles the rats. He cracks it again and again, the sound echoing loudly off the chamber walls. It is the rats that are frightened now. They back away to the far corner of the vast room.

Indy jumps down to the floor and walks over to the chest. He cracks the whip again and sends several rats scampering away. He bends down and begins to work on the chest lid.

The rats begin to come back toward him. He stands and cracks the whip again. Finally he manages to pry the lid of the treasure chest open.

It's empty!

Huntington died for nothing.

Turn to page 48.

Indy raises his whip and lashes out at the fleeing professor.

Huntington ducks away from the whip and runs into the next chamber. Indy is right behind him. They are in the chamber of rats now. The rats screech excitedly and swarm toward the two intruders in their chamber.

Indy leaps onto Huntington's back, knocking him to the ground. The chest bounces onto the hard floor. Rats crawl over both men.

Huntington pulls himself up, kicks away a rat, spies a ledge about six feet off the floor, and tries to climb up to it. Indy slaps away two rats and follows Huntington.

The two men struggle to climb onto the ledge. The rats swarm closer, crawling on each other in their eagerness to grab the men's trouser legs with their filth-ridden claws.

"I'm sorry my men didn't finish you off in the harbor!" Huntington cries. He pushes Indy and sends him sprawling back against the wall.

Indy raises himself up and kicks Huntington with all his strength. Huntington cries out in pain—and falls....

Turn to page 22.

Your ankle hurts. You feel dizzy. But you run into the dark tunnel as fast as you can. And you keep running, until you can't hear the guards coming after you anymore. "I think we lost 'em," whispers Indy. "Hey, wait! What the—!"

He reaches up to a stone shelf and pulls down a small dark object. "The dove!" he gasps. "I don't believe it! Ravenwood must have hidden it in this tunnel! This may be our lucky day after all." He puts the dove carefully into his supply pack.

"But how do we get out of here?" you ask.

It will take even more luck to get you safely out of the tunnel and off Horror Island. Can you do it?

....

If you are reading this book on a Tuesday, Thursday, or Saturday, turn to page 87.

If you are reading this book on a Sunday, Monday, Wednesday, or Friday, turn to page 60. Good luck!

25

"Are you gonna give me a hard time too?" Captain Jim asks, stepping toward you, a crazed look in his one good eye.

"Now, try to calm down," you manage to say, backing away. You listen for Indy, but all you hear is the splashing of the water against the dock piles.

"Maybe you need a swim too!" Captain Jim shouts, reaching forward to grab you.

But Indy has pulled himself back up onto the dock. He grabs the old sailor from behind, lifts him up off the dock, and throws him into the water.

There is a loud splash as Captain Jim hits the water. A few seconds later you hear his frightened cries. "Help me, Jones! Help! You know I'm a terrible swimmer!"

Indy ignores the cries. "He'll get outta there," he mutters. The two of you walk down the dock to the small boat that will take you to Malekula.

What awaits you on the cursed island, the place that's come to be known as Horror Island?

Turn to page 10 to find out.

"Keep running, kid!" Indy cries. "Run all the way to South America if you have to!"

The policeman raises his pistol.

Without slowing his pace, Indy grabs a giant oil barrel at the side of the dock. He gives it a strong push and it rolls right into the policeman. He's pushed over onto his back and his gun flies out of his hand.

Indy grabs the policeman's pistol and keeps running. You're just a few steps behind.

In seconds you're on the deck of the small cargo boat. "We've got to get this crate moving!" says Indy.

Silence.

Suddenly three masked men carrying pistols step out of the captain's cabin. "Where do you think *you're* going?" one of them asks.

Turn to page 58.

"Our friend here seems to have died for a fake," Indy says, shaking his head.

"I don't believe it!" Captain Jim cries as he runs over to Indy. "I just don't believe it!"

Suddenly Indy grabs him in a headlock. "Do you believe that I'm going to break your neck?" Indy growls.

"Wh-what?" Captain Jim struggles to breathe.

Indy tightens his grasp around the old sailor's neck.

"You set this guy up, didn't you, Jim? You planned to get your fee from him—and sell the real dove yourself. You're the only one around who knows this island, and who knew where the dove could be located. You paid off the Malekulans not to interfere. And you planned to walk away from this and retrieve the real carving you've hidden away." Indy squeezes harder on Captain Jim's neck. The old sailor's eyes bulge. His face turns scarlet.

"You—you're real smart, Jones," says Captain Jim, his voice a choked whisper. But somehow the old man manages to pick up a machete from the ground nearby.

"Indy—look out!" you cry.

Will your warning do any good?

....
Turn to page 61.

An armed guard stands at the tunnel opening, his rifle in his hand. "Run into the tunnel!" Indy tells you. "We won't be an easy target in the darkness!"

You run as fast as you can into the blackness of the narrow tunnel. The guard's rifle rings out, but he misses you. You follow the tunnel into an even narrower tunnel, and the rifle shots grow fainter. The guard has lost you—for the moment!

You can hear him in the distance calling for other guards.

"We don't have much time. We've gotta think of—" Indy stops in mid-sentence. "We've got one chance of getting out of here, kid," he says. "Professor Ravenwood left a store of explosives somewhere down here. He and his team used them to dig these tunnels and chambers. If we can find the explosives, maybe we can blast our way out of here—and off the island!"

Will you ever find the explosives in the dark, twisting tunnels? It's all a matter of luck.

Pick a number between one and ten.

If you picked 1, 3, 4, 8, or 9, turn to page 36.

If you picked 2, 5, 6, 7, or 10, turn to page 89.

29

As you reach the main entrance to the excavation, Indy says, "I've got an idea." You both peer out of the opening and see that the natives have gathered at the bottom of the hill. "Let me do the talking," Indy says.

He steps out of the excavation. A cry of surprise rises up from the natives below. The surprise turns to anger. The natives begin to move up the hill. "This doesn't look promising," Indy says, watching the natives approach.

Then one of the natives sees the ebony dove in Indy's hands. The natives begin to murmur as more of them see what Indy is holding.

Then the murmurs become loud cheers. The natives stand and applaud. The cheers and applause echo off the hills for miles around!

You and Indy are heroes for braving the evil of the dark chambers, for challenging the curse of Malekula, and for removing the dove, a symbol of evil for these jungle people.

Indy suddenly has an inspiration. He runs back into the excavation. A few moments later he's back, shooing out hundreds of chickens and roosters—a present for the Malekulans.

The Malekulans promise to row you to New Guinea, where you can begin your trip home. But first you spend the day celebrating—over a dinner of delicious roast chicken!

THE END.

Huntington runs from the chamber, struggling to hold the big chest and his pistol at the same time. But Indy makes no move to follow him. He quickly realizes why you told him to wait.

A few seconds later you hear the anguished cries of Professor Huntington.

He has run right into the chamber of hungry rats.

His screams fill your ears for a few seconds. And then there is silence.

A few moments later you and Indy peer over the low wall and into the chamber. The rats have devoured Huntington. The chest stands in the middle of the floor. There are rats crawling over it, searching for more to eat.

"The dove is all ours," Indy says. "*If* we can get to it."

How can you retrieve the chest from the midst of the rats?

. . . .
Turn to page 49.

You and Indy hit hard ground with a thud. "At least the quicksand was *soft*!" Indy groans. He springs to his feet and begins to explore in the darkness.

"Where are we?" you ask, getting slowly to your knees. "This looks like some kind of tunnel."

"It must be part of Professor Ravenwood's old excavation," Indy says. "I think we've fallen right where we want to be!"

The two of you crawl forward in the darkness until you come to two branching tunnels. On the right you can make out a low, narrow tunnel with gray light flickering from the far end. To your left you can see a larger tunnel, tall enough to stand up in, that twists out of view.

"Well..." Indy says, looking first at one tunnel and then the other. "Which is the shortcut, kid?"

Which tunnel do *you* choose to explore?

....

If you choose the small tunnel on the right, turn to page 42.

If you choose the larger tunnel on the left, turn to page 54.

33

"Keep this gun on them," the man orders Captain Jim, handing him the pistol. "I'll give you a moment with the treasure, Jones. Then I'm afraid it's lights out for you and the kid." He goes into the tent to get the ebony dove.

"Sorry about this, Jones," Captain Jim says. "But I gotta make a living."

Indy scowls but doesn't say anything. The blond man emerges from the tent, the ebony dove in his hands. "I've got two museums bidding for this beauty, Jones. So I know you'll understand why I couldn't let you get here first— and why I can't let you leave here, either. But don't worry, my friend. You won't die a boring death. I plan to make it interesting for you."

He opens the flap to one of the other tents, revealing a large cage. He laughs an evil laugh as he opens the cage door—and out leaps a snarling black panther!

Turn to page 45.

"And where might you be going in such a hurry?" the policeman asks, blocking your path to the cargo boat.

Before you can answer, a shot rings out. The policeman turns away from you and runs off in the direction of the shot.

"That was easy," Indy says as you watch two men in trenchcoats run into the crowd of ships' passengers, pursued by the policeman. "Let's get on the cargo boat before we run into anyone else who's come to see us off."

"Not so fast, Jones!" a voice cries out behind you. "My men did their job well. Now there is no one around but you—and me!"

Turn to page 56.

You stumble through the dark tunnels, moving as fast as you can. You hear angry voices behind you, so you move even faster.

"There it is!" Indy cries. You've found the store of explosives in a small chamber. Indy runs over and picks up a pack of dynamite sticks.

"Stop right there!" a voice calls. Five guards burst into the chamber, followed by four other smugglers.

"Drop your rifles, or I'll blow this whole island off the map!" Indy yells.

The guards stare at Indy, trying to decide whether he's bluffing or not. Indy lights a match and raises it to the fuse of the dynamite pack.

"Let's get outta here! He's nuts!" the leader

of the guards yells. The smugglers and the guards turn and run.

A triumphant smile crosses Indy's face, but suddenly it turns to a look of horror. "Oh no!" he yells. "I accidentally lit this thing!" He drops it to the dirt floor.

The two of you run down the tunnel as quickly as you can. You reach the opening— and daylight—just as the dynamite explodes. The entire store of explosives goes up in a series of mighty blasts.

Badly shaken, you reach the safety of your small boat, and begin your trip home—alive but empty-handed.

Turn to page 95.

Rats are crawling over your shoes, climbing up your pant legs. They drop from the ceiling and land on your shoulder! You kick at them. They back away for a moment and then scramble back to you.

"Fire your gun! Shoot them! Scare them away!" you yell. You slap a rat off your chest, and duck as another one drops off your neck.

"Just stay calm," Indy says. "Stare them down. Step right over them. If you don't panic, they won't attack. We'll be able to walk right through the chamber."

"No! It won't work!" you cry.

How can you get through this rat-infested chamber? You must decide.

If you think Indy should fire his pistol to frighten the rats away, turn to page 79.

If you think you can just stare them down and walk coolly through the chamber, turn to page 112.

"We don't need their help!" one of the mercenaries cries. "Our map will lead us to the dove in the morning. Let's kill these two now before they cause us any more trouble."

"Okay," their leader agrees.

Their rifles blaze, interrupting the quiet of the jungle night. It crosses your mind that you've made a bad decision here. With Indiana Jones around, it's always better to act than to wait. But, unfortunately, you thought of this too late. Your adventure has come to a painfully abrupt

THE END.

"We're only outnumbered thirty to two," Indy says, his eyes surveying the approaching natives. "Let's give 'em a fight!"

He pulls his bullwhip off his shoulder and raises it high in the air.

"Uh...what should I do?" you ask, shivering in your wet clothes.

"Head for the trees on the far edge of this beach," Indy says. "I'll fight 'em off as long as I can. Then I'll join you. We'll lose 'em in the jungle."

You take off, running as fast as you can toward the low, bent trees at the edge of the sand. Indy cracks his whip in the air, but the natives move in. They know that Indy doesn't stand a chance against them.

Crack. Crack. Crack-crack-crack! Rifle fire!

The natives don't have guns. Who is firing the rifles?

Turn to page 53.

"Get back!" Indy yells. "Get back or I'll shoot!"

The furry giant freezes, then backs away. He lifts a big paw and removes the grotesque mask from his face. "Do I know you?" the man asks.

"Higgins!" Indy cries. "What the—"

"Is that you, Jones?" Higgins shouts, a wide grin breaking out over his big, hairless head. "What took you so long? I've been trapped in this hole for five years!"

"But why?" Indy asks. "And where did you rent the snazzy bear costume?"

"I had to come up with a way to keep the Malekulans out of the excavation," Higgins explains. "I was protecting the ebony dove. I knew that Professor Ravenwood would come back for it—and for me!"

"You have the dove?" Indy asks.

"Come. I'll show it to you," Higgins says, lumbering slowly toward the other side of the chamber.

You begin to follow him, but suddenly you hear a loud rumbling.

You look up. The ceiling of the chamber is falling!

Turn to page 55.

"Let's see where that light is coming from," you say.

Indy leads the way on his hands and knees into the low tunnel. The ground feels damp beneath your hands, and the air in the tunnel is thick and musty.

The tunnel leads into another, narrower tunnel, which you squeeze into, crawling forward as quickly as you can.

The light disappears, then appears again. The tunnel twists into another tunnel, which curves and suddenly drops downward.

"Just think—you'll be able to tell your friends how a mole lives," Indy says, crawling ahead of you as you leave one tunnel behind and enter another.

The gray light disappears completely, leaving you in total blackness.

Where will these tunnels lead?

Turn to page 73.

42

Indy spends hours leaning against the rail, his hat tilted back on his head, staring silently into the distance. When he's not doing that, he's sitting in his cabin reading through old books and papers.

One day, after you have been at sea for two weeks, you get him to tell you where you are going and why. "Several years ago Professor Abner Ravenwood led an expedition to the island of Malekula," Indy begins. "He hoped to find the remains of a lost civilization buried in the island. But he failed."

"Why? What happened?" you ask.

"He was chased off the island by the local natives. They claimed that his digging had uncovered ancient evil spirits. Ravenwood and his fellow scientists had to flee for their lives.

"Few have visited Malekula since that time. The natives claim that the island is cursed, that strange creatures roam it and evil spirits haunt what is left of Professor Ravenwood's excavations. They have renamed the island. They call it Horror Island."

"Sounds like a great place to visit!" you say. "Why are we headed there?"

"I'm coming to that part," Indy says.

....
Turn to page 46.

"My little pet is hungry, Jones. Seems he hasn't eaten for a few days, he was so excited about your arrival!" The man laughs, his gold tooth gleaming in the sunlight.

The panther advances quickly, growling loudly, his eyes looking first at you, then at Indy.

You realize that the blond man has made a big mistake. Indy still has his whip and his pistol. The panther moves forward hungrily.

Which should Indy use to fend off the big cat—the whip or the pistol?

The whip? Turn to page 88.
The pistol? Turn to page 7.

The small boat churns its way over the water. Indy leans back against the rail, rolling his coiled bullwhip around and around in his hands, and continues.

"A few minutes after you arrived, I got a call from Marcus Brody. He's the curator of the National Museum. He told me that he'd discovered some papers and a map of Professor Ravenwood's. The papers revealed that just before Ravenwood fled Malekula, he made a fabulous discovery. He uncovered a bird carving, an ebony dove. This dove was worshiped as an idol by the natives of the island more than two thousand years ago. It's absolutely priceless. And it's still on Malekula."

"And your job is to get it for the museum?" you ask.

"To get it for the museum—and to keep it away from all the other jokers who want to get their hands on it. Could be dangerous," he adds, turning serious. "If your parents knew I've brought you along—"

Suddenly you're interrupted by the boat's captain. "This is as far as I can go," he says.

You and Indy turn and look toward the horizon. Off in the distance you see an island. Malekula. "There are no shallows here," Indy protests. "You can bring the boat closer to shore."

"But I *won't*," the captain insists. "There is a curse on the island. This is as close as I go."

Turn to page 67.

Slowly, slowly, stretching with all of your strength, you both reach forward. The long, slender weeds are just inches away from your grasp.

"You're still growing, kid," Indy says. "Now would be a good time to grow another inch or two."

You try once again, leaning forward in the muck, reaching out your fingertips.

You've got them!

Now, pull—*pull!*

You pull with all your might, and the weeds tear out of the soft ground.

"Oh no," you cry, your voice weak from your efforts. "We're right back where we started!"

"No, we're not," Indy says softly. "Look up."

You look up to see that you are surrounded by the army of natives.

Will they rescue you—or let you sink to your death?

Turn to page 57.

"There's a lesson to be learned here," Indy says wryly, "but we don't have time to figure out what it is. Huntington's men must be around here somewhere, and I'd rather not run into them."

You begin to explore other underground chambers of the excavation. After an hour of exploring, you both see the object of your quest at the same moment.

"There it is!" you cry, pointing to a low, flat mound of dirt in the center of a chamber. There stands the dove—unguarded, unconcealed, uncovered.

You start to rush toward it.

"Stop!" Indy whispers.

Suddenly three men carrying guns burst into the chamber. "The dove!" one of them cries, pointing to the statue. They haven't seen you yet.

"Well, Monty, you know what they say about a bird in the hand," one of them says, grinning.

"No. What?" Monty asks, scratching his head.

"Just shut up and grab the dove!" the first one says impatiently. The three men run forward to grab the dove off the mound.

Indy just stands there. Why is he going to let them take it?

. . . .

Turn to page 62.

You and Indy stare at the chest as the rats swarm over it.

"We can't go back in there," Indy scowls. "But we've *got* to get that chest. You didn't happen to bring a pair of stilts, did you?"

You start to answer, but suddenly you get an idea. "Maybe you can lasso the chest and pull it away from the rats," you say.

Indy has his bullwhip off his shoulder before you finish talking. "Good idea, kid. I'm impressed."

He cracks the whip a few times in the air. Rats leap off the chest and scamper back toward the far wall.

Indy raises the whip again, takes aim, and—

FWAAAAAAAAPP!

"Missed!"

He pulls the whip back in.

"This isn't as easy as it looks," he says.

Will he be able to pull the chest out of the rats' chamber?

Turn to page 52.

"I like a refreshing swim before dinner," Indy says, pulling himself up out of the water. "Especially if I'm not the dinner! Too bad you didn't bring your camera, cuz. You'd have some exciting shots to take home to Mom and Dad!"

"Are you kidding?" you cry. "If my parents knew what I was doing right now, they'd kill me!"

"Don't say 'kill,'" says Indy. "We have worse foes to face than those hungry crocs."

It is evening now. The sun seems to drop from the sky in seconds, leaving you in darkness. You continue to walk down the curving banks of the river. The jungle gives way to low, grassy hills. And in one of the taller hills you see a black opening cut out of the dirt.

Professor Ravenwood's excavation!

"We're here, kid," Indy says, wiping his forehead with the back of his hand. "Looks like no one's home. At least they didn't leave a light on for us!"

But Indy is wrong. You hear footsteps. Someone calls out to you. You see a tall figure approaching in the darkness.

Indy grabs his pistol.

Should he shoot or not?

....

If you think Indy should shoot, turn to page 21.

If you think he should wait and see who it is, turn to page 76.

51

FWAAAAPP!

The whip uncoils.

"Missed again." Indy scowls.

He raises his arm and tries once more. This time the whip wraps itself around the chest. Indy pulls back with all his strength. The chest doesn't budge. Rats climb onto the whip.

"Help me," he calls. The two of you pull together. The chest moves an inch. Another inch. It's sliding now. You've got it. One last tug and the chest is in front of you. Indy cracks the air with the whip to scare away the rats.

He pulls open the lid of the chest and reaches inside. "Mission accomplished!" he cries happily. He holds up the ebony dove. "Now we have just one small problem."

"Getting it off this island," you say.

"Well, let's get started," Indy says. "And whaddaya say we try another exit and forget the rats this time?"

"Not a bad idea."

Before long, the two of you have made your way out of the darkness of the excavation and into the sunlight. There waiting for you are several dozen armed natives. You freeze in horror as they raise their weapons.

Turn to page 101.

Suddenly half a dozen men dressed in green army uniforms, carrying automatic rifles, burst out of the jungle. The natives are taken by surprise. Two of them fall to the ground as the men in the green uniforms open fire.

The natives quickly retaliate with their bows and arrows. You and Indy don't wait to see the outcome of this battle. You turn and run into the trees, then push your way through thick, tall grass and leafy vines, into the darkness of the Malekula jungle.

"Who were those men?" you ask Indy, doing your best to keep up with him.

"Probably mercenaries," Indy says without stopping. "My guess is they were hired by someone who wants the idol too."

Soon you come to a river. "We should reach Professor Ravenwood's excavation if we follow the river," Indy says.

A small canoe lies on the sandy bank. "Grab the canoe," Indy says. "It'll get us downriver faster than walking."

"No—let's walk," you say. "I've had enough of water travel for a while. Maybe we'll be safer on land!"

Which way do you choose to travel?

....

By canoe? Turn to page 108.
By land? Turn to page 66.

53

As you step into the tunnel, you choke on the musty air. Falling dust forces you to close your eyes. You stumble forward blindly.

When you open your eyes, you see that you and Indy have followed the tunnel into a vast, open chamber. Your eyes slowly adjust to the dim light.

"What's that chattering sound?" you ask. "What's that scratching?"

Something scurries between your legs. Something crawls over your feet. You feel something crawling up your leg.

You look down at the floor and try to focus. The floor seems to be churning, tumbling, and rolling. But you soon realize that it isn't the floor that's moving—it's the inhabitants of the chamber that are scurrying about—thousands and thousands of rats!

Turn to page 38.

Higgins freezes in terror. You begin to run toward the exit.

"Don't stop, Higgins! Get the dove!" Indy cries. He picks up a wooden support beam from where it has fallen and props it up against the ceiling.

"Hurry! This isn't going to hold it for long!" Indy yells as dirt falls all around him.

"I've got the dove!" Higgins cries.

"Okay—let's get out of here!" Indy yells. The three of you run to the opening at the far side of the excavation chamber and out into the daylight.

"Thank you for doing our work for us," a voice cries out. "You can hand over the dove now."

You are staring at six mercenary soldiers, their automatic rifles poised.

....
Turn to page 113.

"I wish we could stay and chat," Indy says, turning to face a large man with wavy blond hair. "But we're on our way to Hawaii for a little vacation, so—"

The man jabs a pistol into Indy's ribs. "I know where you're headed, Jones. But you're not going there. Some friends of mine have paid me handsomely to see that you sail off in another direction."

"Well, Florida is nice this time of year," Indy says, trying to push the muzzle of the gun out of his ribs.

"The direction I had in mind is *down*," the blond man says with a frown. "Down to the bottom of the ocean. Get moving. You too, kid. This way." He points toward the end of the deserted pier with his pistol.

"I'm not much for deep-sea diving," Indy says, walking very slowly toward the end of the pier.

"Just shut up," the man barks, "and hand over that bullwhip. Right now—no tricks. Understand?"

Indy pulls the bullwhip off his shoulder. He gives you a little wink. You catch his meaning. You throw yourself down to the ground. Indy pulls back his arm and raises the bullwhip in the air....

Turn to page 6.

The natives just stand there and stare down at you as you sink even deeper into the muck.

They murmur amongst themselves. "Please help us!" you cry, your chin sinking into the wet sand. You try to raise your arms up to them, but you can't.

Finally they move. Holding on to each other, they form a human rope. They grab the two of you and slowly, slowly pull you out of the quicksand.

Then they drag you back to their village. They tie your arms and legs with vines and throw you onto the floor of a small, dark hut.

"I think we should've asked for a room with a view," Indy says, his eyes searching the dark room.

"What are they going to do to us?" you ask, struggling against the tightly tied vines.

"Nothing—if I can help it. This looks like some kind of tool shed, kid. If I can crawl over to that shovel, I can use it to cut the vines off my wrists."

Slowly Indy pulls himself over to the shovel and begins to rub the vines against the blade. A few moments later his hands are free. He unties himself and then you.

"Now what do we do?" you ask.

"Now we tie ourselves up again," Indy says. "And we wait for them to come get us."

Has Indy lost his mind?

....

Turn to page 92.

57

"Hit the deck!" Indy screams. You drop to the floor.

Indy grabs the firehose off the cabin wall and turns it on the three masked men. The force of the spray pushes them back, choking and gasping for air.

"Drop your guns and scram!" yells Indy.

The three men don't hesitate. They drop their guns on the deck. Indy keeps the powerful spray on them. They run off the boat and onto the dock.

"Stop where you are!" cries a policeman. The three men are quickly surrounded by cops.

"The cops will be on this boat in no time," Indy says. "I don't know where the crew is, but we've gotta get out of here. We don't have time for explanations."

"We can't sail this boat ourselves!" you cry. You see that three policemen on the dock are heading back in your direction.

"I don't think we have any other choice!" says Indy.

Turn to page 65.

"Stay calm, kid," Indy says. "Try not to move around too much. We'll pull ourselves out of this muck."

Try not to move around?

You've already sunk down to your waist. How can you move around?

"If we stretch just a bit, we can reach those long weeds on the edge of this quicksand pit," Indy says. Then he looks up. "Or how about that low tree branch? Think you could grab hold of it?"

You've got to make a decision—fast! You're sinking lower and lower into the wet, sticky sand.

Do you choose to try for the weeds—or the tree branch?

If you choose the weeds, turn to page 47.

If you choose the tree branch, turn to page 98.

You stumble through the dark tunnel and soon come to the end. You step out into the night.

You find yourselves on the bottom of a low hill at the far side of the excavation. "So far, so good," Indy says quietly, looking around.

But then you see a group of armed guards at the top of the hill. They've spotted you! "Run!" Indy cries. "Head for the beach!"

Zinnnnnng. Zinnnnzinnnnng!

The bullets fly over your head. You run through the trees. You run so hard, your chest feels as if it might explode.

Before you know it, you've left the jungle behind you. You are on the beach. The guards are right behind you at the edge of the trees.

You are trapped!

You cannot swim to safety. You have nowhere to run.

....
Turn to page 85.

Indy squeezes harder. Captain Jim gasps and the machete falls from his hand. "Okay, okay," the old sea captain manages to cry out. "You win, Jones. You win."

A short while later Captain Jim hands over the real ebony dove. And a short while after that, you are on another cargo ship, this time bound for the good old U.S.A.

"Well, this was better than hanging around the house all summer," you tell Indy as the ship carries you over the dark waves.

"Sorry it was a little dull in places, cuz," Indy says wryly. "Maybe next summer we can think of something exciting to do!"

THE END.

As the three men rush forward to grab the ebony dove, they trip a slender thread stretched out in front of the mound.

You hear a cracking sound, a rumble from above, and a slab of granite falls from the ceiling, crushing the dove!

The three men stand staring at the block of granite in disbelief. Then they look up at the ceiling, turn, and run out of the chamber. "I ain't gettin' crushed for no dove!" you hear one of them scream.

"Well...that's the end of the story, kid," Indy says, stepping out from your hiding place.

"Why?" you ask, confused. "The scientists. Why did they set that trap so that it would crush the dove?"

"Professor Ravenwood didn't want it to get into the wrong hands," Indy explains. "Anyone who would rush forward like a fool without checking to see how the dove was being protected didn't deserve to own it."

"But now it's gone for all time," you say.

"No, it isn't," Indy says. He steps over to a wall, measures it with his hands, pulls out a stone, reaches in, and lifts out the ebony dove. The *real* ebony dove.

"Okay, kid, let's go home," Indy says, sounding cheerful for the first time in a month. "Do you want to walk? Or would you rather take a bus?"

THE END.

The scorpion races toward you. You duck away. It just misses your face.

Using the handle of his bullwhip, Indy smashes the huge scorpion before it can come after you again.

You catch your breath for a moment. "Take it easy, kid," Indy says soothingly. "You would've lived for at least another fifteen minutes if that scorpion had bitten you!"

"Thanks, Indy," you manage to say. Then the two of you make your way into the dark tunnel, following it as it curves into a large chamber.

Suddenly you hear another loud howl. You jump back against the dirt wall in fright.

The giant beast-creature has found you!

Turn to page 82.

"Driving a tub like this can't be *that* hard— can it?" Indy asks, looking at the controls.

"Don't we have to lift anchor or something first?" you ask.

"Uh—yeah...I guess so."

But the two of you don't have time to figure it out. You hear the clatter of heavy footsteps on the dock. You and Indy duck down behind a large cargo crate.

Someone—is it the police?—has boarded the boat.

Indy looks around the deck. "We have two choices," he says. "We can jump overboard and wait in the water till they leave. Or we can try to hide down below."

Which do you choose?

If you decide to escape by jumping over-board, turn to page 75.

If you'd rather try to hide aboard the ship, turn to page 14.

65

"There are too many bends and turns in this river," Indy says, looking downstream. "Maybe we'd better just walk along the shore-line after all."

You follow a path that leads downriver. After a mile or so, it veers into the jungle. You have no choice but to follow it. "I think we're getting near the site of the excavation," Indy says.

Suddenly you hear a sound like footsteps—hundreds of them. The jungle floor seems to tremble and vibrate.

Have the Malekulan natives found you already? Have the mercenaries tracked you down?

You step into a clearing. At the other end you see what is making the jungle floor bounce—

WILD BOARS! They're stampeding right at you!

Turn to page 81.

You and Indy are forced to row to shore in a small rubber lifeboat. It flops out of the water, bounces over the high waves, and then hits the surface with a loud smack.

"Hold on to the side, kid. The sea is rough out here," Indy warns.

He doesn't have to tell *you* that!

With every bounce and jolt, you're sure the small lifeboat will tip over and throw you into the churning waters.

And you are right. It does.

"AAAAAIIIII!" You are so shocked you don't even realize that it is *you* doing the screaming! You are pulled into the water, and struggle to float to the top.

"Get to shore! Get to shore!" Indy cries, battling the waves up ahead of you.

The lifeboat bobs off to your right. You look at it—and then at the shore. Should you try to swim to the lifeboat—or to shore?

To the lifeboat? Turn to page 84.
To shore? Turn to page 77.

67

You run up to the opening of the excavation and peer into the darkness, trying desperately to see what happens.

"Drop the dove, Jones—or die in this cave!" the mercenary leader yells.

Indy runs over to the wooden beam that is holding the ceiling up. He pulls the beam away from the ceiling and heaves it at the mercenaries. Two of them are knocked to the ground.

Indy runs toward the excavation opening. The whole ceiling is collapsing now. The roar is deafening.

You hear the screams of the men inside as tons of dirt fall on them. The screams die quickly, and there is silence.

Where is Indy? Was he trapped in there too?

No. He crawls out of the darkness and stands up, handing the precious ebony dove to you.

"I knew this was going to be a dirty job," he says. "But I didn't know *how* dirty! Ready to go home, kid?"

"I guess so," you say with a big smile. "But I have a hunch that home is going to be a little bit boring after this!"

THE END.

"I think we arrived at dinnertime," Indy says, paddling from side to side in the water. You can tell he's trying to figure out how to maneuver away from the approaching crocs.

But the crocs don't give him much room to maneuver. Jaws stretching open to reveal several miles of jagged teeth, a crocodile leaps at Indy. Indy dives backward, and the huge jaws clamp shut on nothing but air.

You duck and dodge as several crocs discover you. You swim away from them, but they come sliding after you. The lead croc is right behind you now and gaining.

Its jaws open wide. You splash and sputter. You turn to face it. Suddenly Indy lifts a giant croc up in both hands—

—and tosses it!

The croc lands on top of the croc about to attack you. The two crocs scramble about in the water, stunned and angry. They fight each other. You hear the *snap snap* of their jaws as you swim to shore.

You've made it!

But has Indy managed to escape the crocs too?

Turn to page 51.

69

"Run!" Indy screams, and he dives right through the line of native soldiers.

They fall back, yelling in surprise. You run to the right, zigzagging across the sand.

"Run! Run!" Indy yells from several hundred yards down the beach.

An arrow whizzes past you, narrowly missing your shoulder. Another. Another.

You hit the ground, roll forward in the sand, get back on your feet, dodge another volley of arrows, roll forward again.

Can you make it to the safety of the trees?

As Indy said, it's all a matter of luck.

Pick a number between one and ten.

If you picked an odd number, turn to page 86.

If you picked an even number, turn to page 97.

Good luck—and keep running!

You crawl through another tunnel and find yourself in a large tunnel that slopes down. The ground becomes sandy, the air hot and moist.

This tunnel takes you into a tunnel that twists and turns uphill. "This is very strange," Indy says. "How could Professor Ravenwood's excavation include all of these small tunnels?"

This tunnel leads to a taller one. You stand for a moment and rub your sore knees. "We must be coming to the end, don't you think?" you ask Indy.

He doesn't answer your question. "Keep moving," he says sharply, entering the darkness of yet another tunnel.

Do these tunnels go on forever?

Turn to page 107.

"Happy landings, kid," Indy says. He climbs up onto the rail and leaps off the boat. You are off the boat before you hear his splash.

You hit the cold water, sink down into the darkness, and then slowly float to the top. You struggle to catch your breath.

Up above, you can hear the policemen searching the boat. "How about down below?" you hear one ask.

"Forget it. It's too dark down there," another cop answers.

Indy smiles as he floats beside you in the water. "These cops are lazy," he whispers. "I think we beat 'em."

Suddenly a bright light shines in your eyes. Two cops with flashlights are standing above, staring down at you. "Hey—look at the big fish down there!" one of them calls to the others, a triumphant grin on his face.

A few moments later you are dragged up by the police. You are going to have a lot of explaining to do. Why are you hiding in the water? Why does Indy have a policeman's pistol?

"This certainly dampens our plans, kid," Indy says dejectedly.

It also ends this adventure with a very bad pun.

Go get a towel and dry off.

Then close this book before you get into any more trouble!

THE END.

75

"Hands up in the air!" the man calls, drawing close enough so that you can see who it is. It's one of the mercenaries in the green uniforms. "This was easier than I thought," he says with a laugh.

"I don't want to make it too easy for you," Indy says, and he punches the man in the stomach. The man falls forward, dropping his pistol.

Indy lands another punch and another.

The man falls to the ground.

"The game is over, Jones," a voice yells from behind you. "Fall to the ground or I'll kill you both."

You turn around to see that the rest of the mercenaries have surrounded you. Their automatic rifles are all pointed at you.

You both fall to the ground.

Turn to page 102.

You decide to swim to land. Luckily, the current helps to pull you toward the shore. Malekula is only a few yards away now.

Gasping for air, you pull yourself up onto the beach. You crawl forward a few feet and collapse onto the sand.

A few minutes later Indy is standing over you, shaking the water from his pistol, his bullwhip wrapped around his shoulder. He pulls you up to your feet and starts to drag you toward the trees at the edge of the beach. Suddenly he stops.

"Uh-oh," he says quietly. "We have visitors."

Turn to page 78.

Still trying to catch your breath, you look up to see a large group of natives approaching. They are heavily armed with long spears and bows and arrows, and they move together as if they were accustomed to protecting their island from intruders.

"Be alert, kid," Indy says. "We may be in for a fight."

You must decide what to do next.

....
If you decide to reason with them, turn to page 91.

If you decide to run into the jungle, turn to page 106.

If you decide to stand and fight them off, turn to page 40.

Click. Click.

Did you forget that Indy's pistol was ruined by your swim in the ocean?

When it doesn't fire, Indy tosses the pistol against the wall in disgust.

There is a moment of silence. And then the cracking noise begins.

You look up to see the wall beginning to crumble. The noise becomes deafening as the dirt wall falls, creating an avalanche, bringing down the ceiling and the other walls.

Thus, this adventure ends with good news and bad news.

The good news is that you found a way to keep the rats from attacking you. You buried them under tons of earth.

The bad news is that you were buried right along with them!

THE END.

Weeks later you stop in a small port in New Guinea to get supplies. From New Guinea it is a few hours' sail to Malekula.

While the supplies are being loaded onto the boat, a tall sailor with a limp approaches Indy. The sailor's face is scarred and twisted, and his left eye stares off into space. "Is that you, Jones, you lubber?" the sailor calls, giving Indy a slap on the back that sends him lurching forward.

"Captain Jim," Indy says, recovering his balance. "I thought they fed you to the sharks years ago!"

"I'm still sailing here and there, mostly there," Captain Jim says, squinting into Indy's face with his one good eye. "Where you headed, Jones?"

"Malekula," Indy says quietly.

"How about taking me along?" asks Captain Jim. "I was there five or six years ago with them scientists. I can show you around."

Indy looks at the old sailor suspiciously. "Quite a coincidence running into you," he says thoughtfully.

Should you take Captain Jim along as a guide?

....

If you say yes, turn to page 90.
If you say no, turn to page 104.

The air turns brown with dust as the wild boars come at you. You stand at the edge of the clearing, not knowing which way to move.

"Seems to be rush hour," Indy says, looking desperately for an escape route.

He pulls out his pistol. "Maybe if I can stop the leaders, the rest will turn around," he says grimly. "It's a slim chance, but…"

Just then you spot a long vine hanging from a tree limb over your heads. "Why don't we climb up onto the vine and let them run under us?" you ask.

"That vine looks weak," Indy says, testing it with his eyes. "You're not as light as you think, y'know."

You must decide what to do—*fast!*

If you think Indy should shoot the lead boars and stampede them in a different direction, turn to page 5.

If you think you have a better chance of surviving by climbing up the tree vine, turn to page 109.

The creature rears up on its hind legs and howls. Its gigantic head looks like—no, it is...

A mask!

In the darkness of the excavation chamber, it's impossible to see clearly. But you're almost certain that the creature howling before you is not an animal at all—but a man in a costume!

Suddenly the giant beast lunges toward you with an angry growl. A massive, fur-covered paw swipes at you and you fall backward.

Indy raises his pistol.

Should he shoot or not?

....

If you think he had better shoot this attacking thing, turn to page 96.

If you think he should try to subdue it without shooting, turn to page 41.

82

Can you swim to the lifeboat? You take a deep breath and start.

Then you realize that the lifeboat is actually coming *toward* you. What a lucky break! Closer and closer it comes, like a gray streak.

You shake your head to get the water out of your eyes. Wait a minute! There seem to be *two* lifeboats coming toward you. Now there are *three*!

And then you stop swimming. You drop your arms and stare. Lifeboats don't have *fins*—do they?

Those gray objects swimming toward you at such speed are sharks—and only hunger could make them swim so fast!

Well...keep ducking those big teeth—and try not to go to pieces! This adventure, sad to say, has come to

THE END.

The guards know they have you trapped on the beach. They advance slowly, their rifles trained on you.

"Hey—over this way!" a husky voice calls.

You see a small motorboat on the water. It's Captain Jim!

"I thought you might need my services after all," the old sailor says. "You're a young hot-head, Jones—but so was I in my time."

You and Indy leap into the motorboat and in seconds you're roaring away from the guards—away from danger, away from Male-kula. "Sorry about what happened back in New Guinea," Indy says. "You're a good friend, Captain Jim." Indy holds up the ebony dove and admires it. "I won't forget this."

"I won't forget any of this adventure either!" you say.

"Well...maybe you'd better forget some parts of it when you describe it to your parents," Indiana says with a chuckle.

As you speed over the water you decide that he's right!

THE END.

OUCH!

OUCH! OUCH!

Get the point?

Sorry to say, that's the problem. You *did* get the point. Several of them. And, of course, those arrows were poison-tipped.

Your luck has run out and so has this adventure. You have just enough time left to read these words:

THE END.

"This tunnel will either lead us out of here, or—" Indy stops. He decides not to finish his thought.

You follow the tunnel as it twists and turns beneath the ground. "If only—" you start to say, but you decide not to finish your thought either. Will your good luck hold out?

No. The tunnel leads you right to the smugglers' headquarters, where several guards await you. Indy reaches for his pistol, but a guard blasts it out of his hand. You are surrounded and outnumbered. There is no escape.

Well...actually...there *is* one way to escape.

Close the book!

The curse of Horror Island has claimed another victim—you! This adventure, sad to say, has come to

THE END.

With lightning speed, the panther leaps at Indy. But Indy is even faster than the sleek animal. His bullwhip slaps away the attacker.

Crack. Crack.

The bullwhip slices the air and the panther leaps backward in surprise. The animal stops and stares at Indy. Everyone seems to freeze.

Then suddenly the panther turns—and attacks the blond man. The attack is short—and fatal. The panther flees into the trees.

You turn away from the hideous sight. Indy bends down and picks up the ebony dove. "Well...it wasn't easy, but it's ours now, kid," he says.

"No, I'm afraid it isn't," Captain Jim says, thrusting his pistol into Indy's back. "I'm afraid you've forgotten one important thing here, Jones—*me!*"

Turn to page 111.

Soon you are lost in the dark, twisting tunnels. "This place has been cleaned out," Indy mutters angrily. "The smugglers did a thorough job, all right."

"How do we get out?" you ask, listening for the footsteps of the guards.

"I'm not sure," Indy says quietly.

Suddenly you hear a voice calling. "They went this way! Over here!"

You've been discovered!

"Forget the explosives!" Indy cries. "Run!"

You start to run, but the ground is soft and wet, and you trip and fall. "Ow!" you cry out in pain. You've twisted your ankle.

"Get up!" Indy yells. "We've reached the main tunnel! Get up! We've got to move!"

Turn to page 25.

"You remember where Professor Ravenwood's expedition was based?" Indy asks Captain Jim.

"I remember every tunnel he dug," the old sailor answers, spitting onto the dock. "I don't know why you want to go into that cursed hole, but I'll take you there, Jones. And my services don't cost much these days."

"Okay, climb aboard," Indy says.

In a short while the cargo boat has brought you to Malekula. You row to shore in a small lifeboat. Several natives are standing on the beach. As you climb out of the boat and strap supplies to your backs, you notice that they pay little attention to you.

"That's strange," Indy says. "These natives don't get many visitors. Why aren't they more interested in us?"

"Pay them no mind," Captain Jim says. He limps off down the beach. "This way, Jones. Follow me."

Indy is still bewildered by the natives' nonchalance. But the two of you follow Captain Jim into the jungle beyond the beach.

Turn to page 20.

"Let me handle this, kid," Indy says, stepping forward to greet the approaching natives. "I've been studying their language. At least, I *think* it's their language!"

Indy raises both hands to show that he doesn't intend to fight. Then he calls out to the leader of the group and says a few words in a strange language.

The natives stare at the two of you in silence, their weapons poised.

Indy continues to talk to them, gesturing with his hands as he talks. It sounds like gibberish to you, but the natives listen intently.

He finishes talking. You both wait to see how the natives react to what he has said.

Neither of you is prepared for their reaction.

They all burst out laughing!

Turn to page 110.

You sit in the darkness with your hands and legs loosely tied. A few hours later four natives enter the small hut and drag you out.

They lead you into a large, candlelit hut that's crowded with natives. "This must be a meeting hall," you think. The whole village seems to be gathered there.

A man in a white robe is chanting at the front of the hall, and the large audience is listening with rapt attention. When the chanting stops, four men push you roughly to the front of the hall.

"There it is!" Indy whispers, indicating the low altar at the front of the hall.

Sure enough, on the altar on a dark wooden stand covered with painted symbols, is the ebony dove!

92

"I knew these natives wouldn't be trying so hard to keep us away unless they had something to protect," Indy says. "Now follow me, kid."

Indy tosses off the loosely tied vines, leaps away from the startled guards, grabs the ebony dove from the altar, and dashes back toward the exit. "Run!" he yells, and you follow right behind him.

Suddenly he trips and falls. The ebony dove flies into the air. You reach for it. You've got it!

Now—run!

Run right on to page 94.

You run with the dove, and Indy is right behind you. "Good fumble recovery, kid," he calls. "Now let's see you outrun their line!"

You turn and see that the entire village is after you.

The two of you twist and turn through the dark jungle trees. Soon you are back on the beach.

"We're trapped!" you yell. "We can't *swim* away from them!"

"There's a canoe!" Indy cries, pointing.

You leap into it, still clutching the dove, and Indy pushes the boat into the water.

You row out into open ocean, the natives watching from the beach. "They won't shoot at us," Indy says. "They don't want any harm to come to the dove."

"Look, Indy!" you cry, your eyes wide in disbelief. "A ship! There's a ship! We're saved!"

You row furiously toward the ship. A short while later you are pulled on board. "This is what I'd call my lucky day," Indy tells the captain. "You can drop us off in any port in New Guinea and—"

"No, I can't," says the captain. "We've just come from there. We're headed to Antarctica. For six months. But don't worry. It may be your lucky day after all. I just might have two extra winter coats aboard!"

THE END.

94

Marcus Brody's office in the National Museum is filled with ancient artifacts, and its oak walls are lined with impressive-looking volumes of archeological studies. He gives an excited cry of surprise as you and Indy walk in.

"You're back!" he exclaims. "Where have you been?"

"Whaddaya mean, where have we been?" says Indy grumpily. "You know where we've been. We've been halfway around the world."

"But I've been trying to reach you for months!" says Brody, jumping up from his desk. "I started right after you left. You see—we have the dove!"

Indy glares at Brody. "What! What are you talking about, Marcus? How could you—"

"We found it. On a bookshelf in Professor Ravenwood's study. You know how careless he always was." Suddenly Brody realizes that Indy is upset. "Sorry, Jones," he says hastily. "I guess your trip was all for nothing, wasn't it?"

Indy's reply is unprintable. As he grows angrier and moves closer to Marcus Brody, you realize it's just as well that this adventure has now come to

THE END.

"Get back!" Indy yells. But the creature does not retreat.

"Get back or I'll shoot!"

The creature responds with an angry roar and leaps at Indy.

Indy fires his pistol once. Twice.

The creature immediately stops its roaring and slumps to the dirt floor. "I'm shot," the creature says softly, in a very human voice, a voice filled with surprise.

It's a man in a costume, just as you had suspected. The man weighs at least four hundred pounds!

You and Indy help pull his mask off. Indy recognizes him immediately. "Higgins!" he cries. "What happened? Why are you here? Why are you dressed like this?"

"Professor Ravenwood will come for me soon," Higgins says, his eyes rolling. "Professor Ravenwood will not leave me here. He will not leave me in these dark tunnels. He will come for me soon."

"He's delirious," Indy says to you. "He must've gone mad, trapped here in this excavation all these years."

"How badly is he injured?" you ask.

"I don't know." But Indy doesn't have time to examine Higgins. The mercenaries have followed you into the chamber!

Turn to page 116.

You roll one more time, arrows cutting the air right above you. Then you're on your feet again, leaping from the sand into the trees.

Your chest aches. You feel as if your lungs are going to burst. But you've made it. The arrows and spears cannot penetrate the dense jungle foliage.

Where is Indy? Did he make it too?

The natives will soon be in pursuit—and they know this jungle much better than you do!

"Hey, kid—this is no time for hide-and-seek!" It's Indy. "How'd you like to see a shooting gallery from the other side?" he asks, guiding you quickly through the low trees.

"I—I didn't," you manage to say.

The two of you keep running deeper and deeper into the jungle. Soon the trees are so thick that no sunlight can reach the jungle floor.

Are the natives following you? You have no desire to turn around and try to see. You just keep running, running until—

Your feet sink into soft, marshy ground. You feel yourself being pulled down into soft, warm slime.

QUICKSAND!

Turn to page 59.

You stretch your arms up as high as they will reach, kicking your legs in the muck, trying to climb up, up, up. "I—I've got the limb!" you cry, grasping it tightly with both hands.

Indy is right beside you. "Can you pull yourself up?" he asks.

Yes, you can. You do.

The two of you move across the low tree limb hand over hand, over the quicksand pit, away from the wet muck that held you captive.

At the end of the limb you drop to the ground.

But when you hit the ground, you don't stop. "Whaaaaa!" you cry in horror as the ground gives way beneath you, and you fall down, down into what seems to be a bottomless pit.

Where will you land?

Turn to page 33.

The rats are circling you now, moving in closer and closer. You keep walking, keep trying to stare them down. But suddenly a rat leaps onto Indy's leg and bites deeply through his trousers. He cries out in pain. Another rat is on him now. And another.

You have almost reached the other side of the chamber. You look down and see that your leg is bleeding. Indy cries out again. You keep walking. The pain in your leg grows stronger, but you struggle to ignore it.

Finally you climb over a low wall at the other end of the chamber. The rats cannot follow you now.

"I guess my little trick didn't work," Indy says, dabbing at a wound with his soiled handkerchief. "We'll try something else next time."

Next time?

You turn around. You are in another large chamber. And there at the far end is a large box. It looks like a pirate's treasure chest.

"That chest just might contain the little item we've been looking for," says Indy.

"You're right. It could!" calls a stranger's voice from the far side of the chamber.

....
Turn to page 11.

The angry natives prepare to attack you and Indy. Then they see the ebony dove cradled in Indy's arm. They grow silent.

Their leader steps forward and talks to Indy in their language. You realize that you are trembling. The natives have you surrounded. There is no escape.

"What's he saying?" you ask. "Are they angry because we're trying to take away the dove?"

Indy grins. "They're pleased as punch, cuz," he says. "This is the happiest day of their lives. They *want* us to take the dove from the island. They believe that the curse on Malekula will be removed once the dove is gone."

"You mean—"

"That's right. They don't know how to thank us!"

"I can think of a *lot* of ways!" you exclaim. "Like, for instance, they could help us get on a boat for home!"

Which is exactly what the Malekulans do, bringing this adventure to a happy

THE END.

"We are reasonable men," the leader of the mercenary group says, his rifle trained on you. "We will not kill you until *after* you show us where the dove is hidden! Ha ha ha!"

"Great sense of humor," Indy mutters, raising his head from the grass. "Why do you want the dove?"

"Don't concern yourself with such details," the mercenary says, giving Indy a hard kick in the ribs. "Don't worry. The museum that hired us will know what to do with the bird."

Suddenly you hear strange cries coming from inside the excavation. The eerie sounds, almost human, float on the wind, then fade.

"Hey—maybe there really is a curse on this place!" says one of the mercenaries.

"Maybe the natives are right. Maybe there are evil spirits on the prowl!" says another.

"These guys aren't so tough," Indy whispers to you. "Get ready. Let's make a run for it."

Has Indy lost his mind? There are five automatic rifles aimed at your heads!

....
If you decide to make a run for it, turn to page 115.

If you think Indy is being a little foolhardy and you should wait for a better opportunity, turn to page 39.

You wait to be lifted onto the ship, your heart pounding. "Stay calm, stay calm," you tell yourself. You wait.

And you wait some more.

It seems like hours.

Finally you can't wait any longer. You push up the lid of the crate and peer out. The dock is deserted.

"Those men are gone!" you tell yourself happily.

But, wait a minute. The other crates that were beside yours—they're gone! And the red cargo boat is gone too!

"Indy—where are you?" you cry. But Indy is nowhere in sight. He was loaded onto the boat!

You look around the empty dock. "This adventure can't be over already—can it?" you wonder.

Yes, it can!

THE END.

"Sorry, old-timer," Indy says, turning away from the old sailor. "Not this trip."

"Wait a minute, Jones. I can be helpful to you. I know a thing or two that you don't!" Captain Jim follows you and Indy down the dock.

"If you know so much, you must know the meaning of the word *no*," Indy says, turning on him.

"I don't have to take that kinda talk from you," Captain Jim says, his face turning scarlet. He gives Indy a hard shove.

"Cut it out," Indy says, walking faster toward the boat. But Captain Jim keeps after him.

He shoves Indy again. And again. "I don't want to fight you, Jim," Indy says, trying to be patient.

"You've insulted me," Captain Jim says, his face still bright red. "Now you gotta fight me."

Captain Jim lunges at Indy and pushes him off the dock and into the water below!

Now Captain Jim turns angrily toward *you*.

....
Turn to page 26.

"I'll fire my pistol in the air to distract them," Indy says, his eyes scanning the jungle trees beyond the narrow beach. "Run to the right, then to the left. Keep moving from side to side. They won't be expecting us to run. With any luck, we can lose them in the trees."

With any luck!

The natives approach. Several bow carriers raise their weapons as they walk, pulling arrows from long quivers.

Indy quickly reaches into his pocket and pulls his pistol out. He raises it into the air and squeezes the trigger.

Click.

Click. Click.

It seems that ocean water has not done Indy's pistol any good.

Now what?

Turn to page 72.

This tunnel leads into a cool, moist tunnel that slopes down into another tunnel. You crawl forward wearily. You know you've come too far to turn around. You could never find your way back anyway!

Indy cuts a jagged line into the side of the tunnel with his knife. "I want to see if we're going around in circles, kid," he says.

He crawls forward, following the twists and turns of the next low tunnel of darkness.

Is it possible that you are going around in circles? Can you be trapped in this bizarre labyrinth of tunnels—forever?

Turn to page 73.

"Come on, sport," Indy says, giving you a little shove toward the canoe. "This river is as gentle as a bathtub!"

Before you know it, you are sitting across from him, watching the gentle water flow by as he rows you downriver...watching the gentle water flow faster...start to churn...start to get choppier and choppier!

Suddenly the canoe flies into the air and falls back down to the water with a loud slap. "Hmmm," Indy says, "must be an ocean inlet or something. I've never seen a river that—"

He doesn't finish his sentence because the canoe tips over!

Turn to page 114.

Indy was right.

You're not as light as you think.

You and Indy pull yourselves up the vine as the hideous creatures roar toward you.

The vine breaks. You fall back to the ground. The wild boars are upon you now.

You really don't want to know what happens next, do you? Better close the book before you are forced to think about the gruesome details of how your adventure came to

THE END.

"What did you say to them?" you ask Indy as the native army continues to laugh.

Indy scratches his head. "I *think* I told them the real reason we came here—to find the ebony dove carving in the excavation left by Professor Ravenwood. I don't know the language that well, but..."

When the natives stop laughing, their leader beckons for you to follow them. They seem much more relaxed. They carry their weapons jauntily at their sides, and every few steps they burst into laughter.

They lead you through the jungle, down a carefully worn path to a village built on the site of the old excavation. The entrance to the excavation is still intact, and the native soldiers lead you through it, into a vast cavern. It must have been dug by the scientists many years ago.

Filling the floor of the cavern, as far as you can see, are hundreds and hundreds of carved ebony doves!

Turn to page 118.

Indy may have forgotten about Captain Jim's presence—but Captain Jim has forgotten about you.

He doesn't see you as you creep up behind him. You pick up speed and barrel into him. He falls forward, his face hitting the dirt.

Indy grabs the pistol. Captain Jim is no longer a threat.

"Nice goin', cuz," Indy says. "I can really tell now that we're related. You're just as reckless as I am!"

And with that fine compliment, this adventure has come to

THE END.

The rats scratch at your legs and scamper over your shoes as slowly, slowly you begin to walk through them.

"Stop shaking like that, cuz," Indy says. "The secret is to show them no fear." He swats a chattering black rat off his head.

A group of rats behind you start to screech, a high-pitched whistling that sends shivers up and down your back. "No fear, no fear, no fear," you repeat over and over to yourself.

Suddenly your foot hits a rock. You trip. You catch yourself and pull yourself back up onto your feet, shaking rats off your back and shoulders.

"No fear, no fear," you repeat, staring the rats in the eyes as you step over them. You walk slowly, carefully—so slowly that you think you'll never make it to the other side.

Finally you reach the center of the chamber. There are rats all around you in a chattering, scratching, scampering circle.

"Stare them down!" Indy cries as a hungry rat takes a swipe at his leg with long, yellow teeth. Indy kicks the rat aside and keeps walking.

"No fear, no fear," you tell yourself as you slowly move forward through this thick carpet of rats.

Turn to page 100.

"Hand over the dove, Jones," the leader of the mercenaries yells, reaching for it. "Don't worry. You'll get a nice reward—a thank-you note from the museum that hired us!"

Indy grabs the dove out of Higgins's hands.

"If you clowns want the dove, you'll have to come get it!" Indy yells.

And he runs back into the excavation.

The mercenaries can't decide what to do for a moment. Then they rush into the dark cavern after him.

Will anyone come out alive?

Turn to page 68.

You're swimming for your life again!

You take a deep breath and struggle to stay on top of the tossing waves. The current sweeps you downriver. You're pulled underwater, struggle to the surface again, and sputter for air.

"This is even faster than riding the canoe!" Indy calls from about fifty yards away. *Very funny!* You hope you'll be alive to laugh about it later.

Then, before you realize what's happening, the waves die down and the current slows. The water becomes gentle again.

"We're going to make it!" you yell. "We're going to make it!"

Then you see the crocodiles swimming toward you.

Turn to page 69.

Indy leaps to his feet and throws a handful of wet dirt into the eyes of the mercenary leader. He lowers his shoulder and plows into another mercenary, knocking him into two others.

You run toward the excavation, tripping in the dark, crawling partway. You can hear Indy's footsteps behind you.

And you can hear the *ratatatatat* of automatic rifle fire. The bullets fly around you as you run, run through the darkness toward the even darker opening of the excavation.

The mercenaries keep firing in your direction. But they cannot see you in the dark. You reach the opening of the excavation. You leap inside.

The ground is cold and soft. You are in a large, empty chamber. Empty except for the eerie cries in the distance. Empty except for the loud flapping noises you now begin to hear, the sound of killer bats whose rest has been disturbed!

Turn to page 3.

"Back away from there slowly, Jones," the leader of the mercenaries says, holding his automatic rifle in front of him. "It's time for you to lead us to the dove."

"Professor Ravenwood will be back for the dove," Higgins cries in a voice growing weaker by the moment. "He will come back for me."

"Back away, Jones—fast!" the mercenary cries, fingering the trigger of his rifle. The other mercenaries aim their rifles at you too.

You and Indy start to back away from the giant Higgins, who lies bleeding at your feet. Suddenly Higgins lifts his right arm. He reaches for the wall.

His hand tightens around something—a lever! He pulls it.

"Aaaaaiiiieeee!" the mercenaries scream as the floor opens up beneath them. The lever has opened a huge trap door. The mercenaries fall below and the floor closes above them.

Higgins has saved your lives.

You rush over to see how badly he is injured.

Go on to page 117.

You and Indy pull away Higgins's furry disguise.

"My costume," Higgins says weakly. "I wore it to keep everyone away. I'm waiting for Professor Ravenwood. I have the dove. I know he wants it."

His wounds are not serious. "You're going to be okay," Indy tells him. "We'll get you to the mainland and to a doctor."

"Professor Ravenwood," Higgins mutters. "Get me to Professor Ravenwood."

"Where is the dove?" Indy asks.

"I have it," Higgins says. "I have it here. I carry it in my costume." He attempts to sit up, but he is too weak. He reaches into the costume of pieced-together furs. "Oh no. No!"

He pulls out a handful of black wood chips.

"When I fell, I—I—crushed it!" Higgins cries.

The priceless ebony dove is now mostly splinters.

You and Indy look at each other. You've come a long way and faced many dangers to get to this—splinters!

"It could've been worse, kid," Indy says. "*You* could've been the one to break it! Now, let's get outta this place. I feel real homesick all of a sudden!"

THE END.

"Pinch me, kid. I've gotta be dreaming!" Indy cries.

Seeing your surprise, the natives start laughing again. The leader begins to talk rapidly to Indy, who struggles to understand him.

Finally Indy translates for you. "The natives discovered the dove down here after Professor Ravenwood fled," he explains. "It still held a special power for them. The people of the island decided to duplicate it, to fill the excavation cavern with them. Now there are hundreds of them—maybe thousands! We're staring at the biggest collection of carved doves in the world! Great, huh, kid?" says Indy.

"What about the original?" you ask.

Indy shakes his head. "It's in there somewhere. Care to start looking for it? I'll join you in a year or two when you start to get bored!"

You turn down Indy's generous offer. A few hours later the two of you are on a boat heading for New Guinea. From there you'll begin your journey back to the United States.

"Here, have a souvenir," Indy says. He pulls something out of his jacket and tosses it to you. You don't have to look. You know what it is. It's an ebony dove!

"Indy, you shouldn't have!" you say.

"I know! I know!" he says grumpily. Then he turns to watch the dark ocean waves roll by as your ship heads toward home, bringing this less than successful adventure to

THE END.

118

To Pip (Andrea, Jr.)

... because we are all holding each other
through a dance of joy and love.

Hug often —
love,
Aunt Andi (Andrea, Sr.)

This is a book about hugging.

Hugging is an instinct, a natural response to feelings of affection, compassion, need, and joy.

Hugging is also a science, a simple method of support, healing, and growth, with measurable and remarkable results.

In its highest form, hugging is also an art.

Techniques of hugging are described here with a cheerful mix of whimsy and seriousness. May they serve as a framework for you to create your own experience and practice as a Hug Therapist.

THE
HUG THERAPY
BOOK

(Kathleen Keating)

Drawings by Mimi Noland

HAZELDEN®

INFORMATION & EDUCATIONAL SERVICES

Hazelden
Center City, Minnesota 55012-0176

Cover and interior design by Kristen McDougall

ISBN: 1-56838-094-1

I embrace with honor

My daughter, Ann Maureen Keating,
and all those at her special place of learning
for the developmentally disabled,
St. Vincent School in Santa Barbara, California

and my son, Matthew Roy Keating

I embrace with gratitude

Golda Clendenin, who inspired me

My friends and colleagues at Woodview-Calabasas
Hospital, who supported me

Esalen Institute for teaching me

David Gorton for believing in me

hug (hug) v.t. hugged, hugging, hugs.

    1. to clasp or hold closely, especially in one's
      arms; embrace or enfold, as in affection
    2. to cherish, hold fast
    3. to keep very close to

hug n.

An affectionate embrace. (From Scandinavian,
akin to old Norse *hugga*, to comfort, console.)

hug therapy

The practice of administering hugs for the purpose
of curing or healing, or of preserving health.
Treatment of dis-ease through the simple, physical
means of hugging.

About hugging and huggers

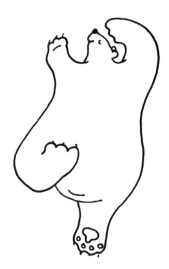

A hug makes you feel good all day.

Theory

Touch is not only nice. It's needed. Scientific research supports the theory that stimulation by touch is absolutely necessary for our physical as well as our emotional well-being.

Therapeutic touch, recognized as an essential tool for healing, is now part of nurses' training in several large medical centers. Touch is used to help relieve pain and depression and anxiety, to bolster patients' will to live, to help premature babies — who have been deprived of touch in their incubators — grow and thrive.

Various experiments have shown that touch can:

Make us feel better about ourselves and our surroundings;

Have a positive effect on children's language development and IQ;

Cause measurable physiological changes in the toucher and the touched.

We are just beginning to understand the power of touch.

While there are many forms of touching, we propose that hugging is a very special one that contributes in a major way to healing and health.

Rationale

HUGGING

Feels good

Dispels loneliness

Overcomes fears

Opens doors to feelings

Builds self-esteem ("Wow! *She* actually wants to hug *me!*")

Fosters altruism ("I can't believe it, but I actually *want* to hug that old son-of-a-gun!")

Slows down aging; huggers stay younger longer

Helps curb appetite; we eat less when we are nourished by hugs—and when our arms are busy wrapped around others

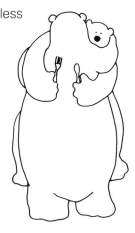

HUGGING ALSO

Eases tension

Fights insomnia

Keeps arm and shoulder muscles in condition

Provides stretching exercise if you are short

Provides stooping exercise if you are tall

Offers a wholesome alternative to promiscuity

Offers a healthy, safe alternative to alcohol and other drug abuse *(better hugs than drugs!)*

Affirms physical being

Is democratic; anyone is eligible for a hug

HUGGING ALSO

Is ecologically sound, does not upset the environment

Is energy-efficient, saves heat

Is portable

Requires no special equipment

Demands no special setting; anyplace from a doorstep to an executive conference room, from a church parlor to a football field, is a fine place for a hug!

Makes happy days happier

Makes impossible days possible

Imparts feelings of belonging

Fills up empty places in our lives

Keeps on working to dispense benefits even after the hug's release

Besides, hugging prevents war.

Qualifications

The qualifications for being a Hug Therapist and being a client are the same: just being.

Therapeutic hugging is a mutually healing process. In fact, hugger and hugged play interchangeable roles. As a Hug Therapist, you are open to the child within you who needs love, safety, support, caring, and play, and you are reaching out to the same needs in the other.

A Hug Therapist does not blame or judge. But he or she does recognize that many of us, in our standoffish society, have not learned to ask for the emotional support we need. If love or support—or play—has been skimpy since childhood, we may feel wounded. If the twistings of growing up have left us with low self-esteem, we may feel unlovable—unhuggable.

Hug Therapists can't solve all these problems, but they can respect the struggles and offer understanding, laughter, gentle words, and an abundance of hugs.

Hug Therapy is not just for the lonely or hurting ones. Hug Therapy can make the healthy healthier, the happy happier, and the most secure among us feel even more so.

Hugging is for everybody.

Anyone can be a Hug Therapist. But if you master the Types of Hugs and the Advanced Techniques presented in this book, you will develop further skills and confidence in your natural ability to share wonderful hugs.

Ethics and rules of conduct

When you are a truly professional Hug Therapist, you take full responsibility for what you say or do. Therefore the hugs you share must be thoughtful, respectful, and care-filled.

These are understood rules of conduct for Hug Therapists:

1. *Since Hug Therapy is always nonsexual, hug accordingly.* Be sure that the hugs you dispense are compassionate, not passionate. A caring, comforting, or playful hug is different from a lover's embrace. We usually recognize the difference.

No.

If you started out offering or wanting a supportive hug, and it has taken on overtones of greater physical intimacy, just recenter your feelings and thoughts on the original purpose of the hug—to give mutual support.

If you are clear about the kind of hug you are giving, the other hugger most likely will respond in kind. If not, you may want to have a talk about the importance of just-friendly hugs in your relationship.

Yes.

2. *Be certain you have permission before giving a hug.* Often permission to hug is implicit in a relationship. Your sweetheart or a close friend probably will welcome hugs almost any time. However you still need to respect the other's need for privacy and space.

Sometimes you will receive nonverbal permission from someone who wants a hug, and you respond spontaneously. Or pave the way to hugging with a simple comment like, "I would like to give you a hug." Respect the other's verbal and nonverbal messages. Most of the time you will be aware of what is needed and acceptable.

If you misread someone who did not find a hug comfortable, don't be concerned. For some, hugging is very hard; sometimes a sturdy trust must be built before they feel safe enough to hug. Although we Hug Therapists believe the gift of touch to be extremely important, the gift of acceptance is just as important!

Ask first.

3. Also be sure to ask permission when <u>you</u> need a hug. Hug Therapists are not only dispensers of hugs but recipients too. Huggers must sometimes be huggees. Hugging-for-health is a practice of sharing, rather than of just giving or just taking.

When you feel the need for a hug, say: "I would like a hug, if it's all right with you." Or, "I could really use a huge hug right now—would you oblige?" Or, "How about a hug before I go off to work (or to a meeting or a match or an interview or whatever). A post-hug "thank you" or "that felt good" is an important validation of the other's support.

May I have this hug?

4. *Be responsible for expressing what you need and the way you want it.* Blaming others because we're not getting what we need from them is a common mistake we make in our relationships. Some are naturally fine-tuned and intuitive about others' needs and comforts. But most of us—especially if we are busy worrying about our own insecurities—need direct, explicit communication.

If we want more hugs, fewer hugs, ten-second hugs, or two-minute-over-easy hugs—any kind of hug that may be different from what we're getting—we need to say so. Then we have to be willing to compromise as well as to realize that we won't always get exactly what we want when we want it.

For some, hugging is very hard.

Contraindications

A MYTH AND A MODEL

While Hug Therapists are convinced that hugging is for everyone, a few doubters have trouble accepting Hug Therapy. They believe, erroneously, that the sole purpose of a hug is to build a relationship of physical intimacy.

A physically intimate embrace can be beautiful too, but it meets a different level of need. This kind of embrace will never replace a good old therapeutic hug! Even intimate partners need bundles of ordinary hugs too.

To keep little ones from acquiring this narrow view of hugs, hug them often—affectionately, supportively, playfully, and tenderly. Let them see parents and other adults hugging in these ways. Otherwise they may grow up believing that hugs are for lovers only, and that in order to be hugged—and huggable—one must be physically attracted to the other hugger.

A Hug Therapist makes every effort to share the broader understanding of touch and hugging and the faith that a day filled with hugs can bring untold satisfaction and serenity.

Fees

Hug Therapy is not free. The cost is the strength it requires to be vulnerable. The fee for hugging is the risk that our hugs will be rebuffed or misinterpreted.

When we are very young we are naturally open. We want to give love and touch as much as we want to get love and be touched. If we're deprived of love and touch, we become unwilling to pay the fee of vulnerability. Love held back can turn to pain.

Hug therapists can help ease this pain. When we risk our hugs, we affirm our wonderful ability to share. As we reach out and touch others, we are free to discover the compassion — along with the capacity for joy — that exists in all of us. As we become more spontaneous huggers and find such inner riches, the fees seem relatively small.

Thank goodness we have our softer sides.

Types of hugs

Bear hug

In the traditional bear hug (named for members of the family Ursidae, who do it best), one hugger usually is taller and broader than the other, but this is not necessary to sustain the emotional quality of bear-hugging. The taller hugger may stand straight or slightly curved over the shorter one, arms wrapped firmly around the other's shoulders. The shorter of the pair stands straight with head against the taller hugger's shoulder or chest, arms wrapped—also firmly!—around whatever area between waist and chest that they will reach. Bodies are touching in a powerful, strong squeeze that can last five to ten seconds or more.

We suggest you use skill and forbearance in making the hug firm rather than breathless. Always be considerate of your partner, no matter what style of hug you are sharing.

The feeling during a bear hug is warm, supportive, and secure.

Bear hugs are for:

Those who share a common feeling or a common cause.

Parents and offspring. Both need lots of reassuring bear hugs.

Grandparents and grandoffspring. Don't leave grandparents out of family bear hugs.

Friends (this includes marrieds and lovers, who hopefully are friends too).

Anyone who wants to say, wordlessly, "You're terrific!" Or, "I'm your friend; you can count on me." Or, "I share whatever pain or joy you're feeling."

What can a bear hug say for you?

The A-frame hug

Stand facing each other, wrapping arms around shoulders, sides of heads pressed together and bodies leaning forward and not touching at all below shoulder level. There. You have an A-frame hug. The length of time spent in the A formation is usually brief, since this is often a "hello" or "goodbye" hug.

The underlying feeling may be one of polite caring or detached warmth.

The A-frame hug is most appropriate for new acquaintances or professional colleagues, or in situations that require a degree of formality. Because it is relatively nonthreatening, it is comfortable for shy or unpracticed huggers.

This is a classic hug and should not be discounted because of its formal quality. It has broad application and is therefore beneficial to a wide range of huggers.

An A-frame hug is particularly apt for:

A great-aunt whom you haven't seen since you were a toddler.

Your spouse's employer's husband.

Your former academic adviser.

A new daughter-in-law.

Who else?

Like this.

Cheek hug

The cheek hug is a very tender, gentle hug that often has a spiritual quality. It can be experienced comfortably sitting down, standing up, or even with one sitting and one standing, as full body contact is not necessary.

If you are both seated, turn comfortably toward each other and press the sides of your faces together cheek to cheek. One hand may be on the other's back and the other supporting the back of the head to counteract the pressure of your cheek. Breathe slowly and deeply. Within a few seconds you will feel very relaxed. The cheek hug often stirs deep feelings of kindness, especially when participants are close friends.

A cheek hug is a tasteful way to:

Greet an elderly friend or relative who is seated.

Say a wordless "I'm sorry" about a friend's disappointment.

Share a friend's joy at a happy occasion, like a wedding or graduation. (This is a considerate hug for congratulating the principals in reception lines, since it does not tangle wedding veils or crush boutonnières.)

At what times would you proffer a cheek hug?

It often has a spiritual quality.

Sandwich hug

The sandwich hug is a lesser known variety, but once you experience its warmth and security, you'll want to share this one often.

This is a hug for three. Two face each other with the third in the middle facing either one of the others. Each of the two on the outside reaches toward the waist area of the other and hugs. The one in the center wraps arms around the waist of the facing hugger. As an option, the outside pair may hug around the shoulders and all three snuggle heads together. The bodies are touching cozily.

The sandwich hug gives the one in the middle an especially secure feeling, which is helpful if she or he is going through a difficult time and needs extra support.

The sandwich hug is handy for:

> Three good friends.

> A couple wishing to comfort someone.

> Two parents and a child. The child may be very young, grown up, or any place between.

Make your own sandwich.

Grabber-squeezer hug

The grabber-squeezer hug holds the record for brevity. One hugger runs up to and throws arms about another, gives a fast squeeze before letting go, then dashes off. The one so hugged must be alert in giving a squeeze in return, in order to receive maximum benefit from this hug.

In a variation of the grabber-squeezer, choreographically more difficult, both run toward each other and give a quick, simultaneous squeeze. Safety note: Avoid a collision course. The full-force crash of two bodies who have hurtled together or the knocking of two heads may negate some of the good feelings!

Feelings vary with the situation, but often the grabber-squeezer is accompanied by a sense of affectionate

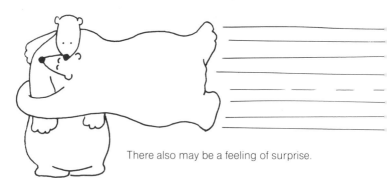

There also may be a feeling of surprise.

distraction because one or both of the huggers are rushed. If the huggee is not expecting it, there also may be a feeling of surprise.

Grab-and-squeeze hugging is a practical way to work in a lot of fast hugging when you're on a tight schedule. For more effective stress management, also include a liberal sprinkling of hugs that are gentler and last longer.

Use the grabber-squeezer:

    In the workshop or the kitchen.

    To wish someone luck before a performance.

    As a silent translation of the words "I like you a lot, but I'm in a terrible hurry!"

How can the grabber-squeezer fit into your life?

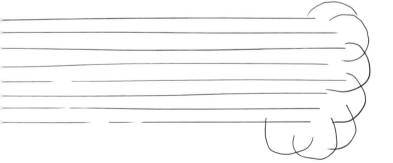

Group hug

The group hug is a very popular hug for good friends sharing in an activity or project. As Hug Therapists, we would like the group hug to be better known and more often applied, just because it feels so good.

The group forms a circle — its members standing as close together as possible, arms around shoulders or waists — and squeezes. In a variation, group hug participants, holding each other as above, move in toward the center, shrinking the circle. They huddle together for several moments, then back up and break apart with a cheer or sigh or a quick, parting squeeze.

Besides good feelings of support, security, and affection, group hugs often impart a sense of unity and universal belonging.

Group hugs are good for:

    Growth groups.

    Support groups.

    Classmates, teammates.

    Hardworking committees.

    Any bunch you like.

When would your group welcome a hug like this?

A group hug often imparts a sense of universal belonging.

Side-to-side hug

The side-to-side hug, or the lateral squeeze, is a great hug to get and give while walking along together. As you stroll side by side with an arm around the other's waist or over the shoulder, once in a while give a generous squeeze.

This is also a merry and playful hug for those moments when you are standing in line with a friend. It makes queuing up a pleasure!

The side-to-side hug provides a joyful moment while:

Walking to a bus.

On a hike or an archaeological dig.

Waiting to get into a Saturday night movie or to register for next term's classes.

When could you use a side-to-side hug?

Back-to-front hug

In the back-to-front hug (also known as the waist-grabber), the hugger approaches the other from the back, folds arms around his or her waist and gives a gentle hug.

The back-to-front waist-grabber is the perfect hug to give someone who is peeling potatoes, scrubbing pans over a kitchen sink, or otherwise engaged in some routine stand-up chore. A somewhat old-fashioned hug, this was practiced more extensively before the invention of the automatic dishwasher. But most of the time a waist-grabber is still welcome as a brief, playful gesture. The feeling behind it is happy and supportive.*

*Even more supportive would be the back-to-front hug *followed by* the picking up of a dishtowel and applying it to the pans.

Back-to-front hugs are for:

Househusbands, housewives, and other live-ins.

Co-workers on an assembly line.

Friends whose occupations require that they face
mostly in one direction—like raspberry-pickers
or mail-sorters.

*Do you know someone who would appreciate a
waist-grabber?*

Heart-centered hug

Many consider the heart-centered hug to be the highest form of hugging, and official Hug Therapists feel, too, that it is indeed very powerful.

The heart-centered hug begins with direct eye contact as the two huggers stand facing each other. Then the arms are wrapped around shoulders or back. Heads are together, and there is full body contact. The hug is firm, yet gentle. As the two breathe slowly and easily together, they focus on the compassion that is flowing from one heart into the other.

There is no time limit on this hug; it may last several moments, shutting out all nearby distractions. The heart-centered hug is full and lingering, caring and tender, open and genuine, supportive and strong.

The heart-centered hug acknowledges that place at the center of each of us where—if we're open to it—pure, unconditional love may be found.

The heart-centered hug feels right:

When the huggers are very old friends with a long history of crisscrossing paths.

When the huggers are very new friends brought together by a shared experience and a strong, shared emotion.

When might you share a heart-centered hug?

It may last several moments, shutting out all distractions.

Custom-tailored hug

The most effective hug for you is the hug that feels right, considering the setting, the situation, the one you are with, and what you personally need from the hug (affection, strength and support, reaffirmation of a bond of friendship, relaxation, or any other good feeling that a hug can bring.)

Sometimes a custom-tailored hug is called for, as in the case of an extra-tall hugger and a very short huggee (or vice versa). Or when the hug, in order to please both parties equally, has to include a jealous pet or a favorite toy too.

Be creative. True Hug Therapists do not let circumstances stand in their way.

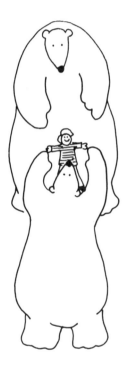

A custom-tailored hug may have to include a favorite toy.

Hugs: where, when, why

Environments

A place of beauty enhances the experience of hugging. Whatever setting you consider beautiful—a peaceful country path on a warm, clear day or a scrap of green park that opens a city to the sky—can make the hug you share with a friend even more special.

However, if the setting seems shabby or bleak, it can be totally transformed just because you are sharing a hug.

Anyplace is the right place for hugging when the heart is open.

A hug transforms a bleak setting...

...into a lovely place.

Time of day

Some are morning, up-and-at-'em huggers. Some are evening, thank-heaven-the-day-is-over huggers. Some like to hug at high noon on lunch hours or at teatime. Although routine hugs are fine, sometimes the most appreciated hugs happen spontaneously at unexpected moments.

The feelings that bring on a hug — affection, sympathy, caring, just plain joy — can happen at any time of day. So can hug situations, like bumping into an old school friend at an airport. True Hug Therapists will entertain the idea of a hug at any time. And hugs scattered through the day will help to maintain a sense of well-being, belonging, and self-esteem.

Friendship

Compassion

Joy

Feelings that bring on a hug . . .

...can happen any time.

Sound effects

A hug may be accompanied by a moment of stillness.
Or it may include expressions of pleasure, like these:

(Sigh)

Whoopee!

That's nice.

Thank you. I needed that.

Advanced techniques

Visualization

Visualization is a powerful technique for learning and change. One way we learn is through repeated imprintings on our minds—not only of what we actually view in the world around us, but also of pictures we see in our imaginations. Imagined pictures, which can affect us as strongly as reality, sometimes even set off physical responses.

Think about slicing a juicy lemon and squeezing the tart juice into your mouth. Your mouth waters at the very thought. You may detect a sour taste, too. You have the sensation of sucking a lemon even though there's no real lemon anywhere in sight.

Now try visualizing yourself hugging somebody. Let this imagined hug register in your mind as a nourishing experience. A mind picture like this can teach you to see yourself as someone who is at ease giving and getting warm, caring hugs.

In guided imagery, you plan or guide the direction you'd like your imagination to take. So let's say you would like to be comfortable greeting a friend with a heart-centered hug. Sit in a comfortable, quiet place and close your eyes. Breathe slowly and deeply four or five times and let your body relax totally. Imagine yourself walking along and meeting a good friend. Picture the two of you saying hello by putting your arms around each other and sharing a heart-centered hug.

Keep the picture in your mind as you sense good feelings of affection and warmth. It is important to put the imagined picture and the feelings together.

Or use guided imagery when you are feeling the need for support after a stressful day. Visualize a favorite friend who is also a good hugger giving you a very fond and supportive hug. Imagine that friend holding you and offering you reassurance and love. Keep the picture and the feelings in your mind for as long as you need comfort.

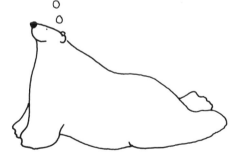

An imagined hug is a nourishing experience.

Zen hugging

You can use any type of hug for Zen hugging. Our favorites are the cheek-to-cheek hug or the heart-centered hug. A very connected touch — a feet-to-feet and hands-to-hands touch, for instance — will do fine, too.

Your eyes may be open or closed. Focus on your breathing, and allow it to become even and deep. You will begin to feel yourself relaxing. You are centered in the present moment. Let go of all thinking. All that is present is the experience of your senses.

You are aware of the warmth you are sharing, of your breath moving in and out, of the touch of the other person, of the air on your skin. Relax. Be suspended in time. The longer you are able to relax in the present moment, the deeper will be your experience of the hug or the touching.

Peace.

You are centered in the present moment.

That extra touch

Hugging is just one kind of therapeutic touching. There are others too, as touch research has confirmed.

You may want to combine hugging with another nourishing kind of platonic touching, such as gentle stroking or patting.

There are other kinds of therapeutic touching too.

Institute of hug therapy

We believe more must be done to break down the cultural and emotional barriers that prevent us from experiencing the healthy nourishment of touching and hugging. The establishment of the Institute of Hug Therapy is our whimsical, but earnest, contribution to that effort.

Becoming a member of the Institute of Hug Therapy is easy. Just believe in the power of hugging! Wear the title of Hug Therapist proudly. Tell others about hugging for health. Spread the pro-hug philosophy wherever you go.

Hugging should not be something you do once in a while, at family reunions or birthdays or when one of your teammates makes a goal. Our hope is that hugging will become commonplace, without detracting from the specialness of each separate hug.

Institute of Hug Therapy
Certificate of Membership

This is to certify that

_____
name

has completed the course of study offered in *The Hug Therapy Book* and is now a practicing Hug Therapist dedicated to the furtherance of hugging for health on an international scale.

Hug often. Hug well.

About the author

Kathleen Keating Schloessinger, R.N., M.A., is a mental health educator, consultant, and counselor in private practice. She also conducts seminars and workshops worldwide on "The Power of Touch," "The Nature of Love and Intimacy," "Translating the Heart: Creative Self-Analysis," and "The Wounded Healer." Her experience also includes work in the areas of stress management, communication and problem-solving skills, and group dynamics. She and her husband, Fred Schloessinger, a psychotherapist, live, love, and work together in Guelph, Ontario, Canada

The theme of her life is, she says, "to feel, know, and teach the many dimensions of love: courage to struggle; vulnerability to give and to receive; sensitivity to compassion and the power of anger; openness to the delight of play and the deep, deep pleasure of a warm embrace."

"I want a world where people are respected for the ease and warmth of their melting... rather than the strength of their walls."

Clint Weyand
from *My Miracle Is You*
(Being Books)

"Since our beginnings we have been acquiring knowledge and wisdom. We have been Homo Sapiens—knowing human. Now we have enough new knowledge to enter our next dimension, as Homo Biologicus—biological human. What does our biological organism require to function at its optimum, its most joyful? We now have scientific evidence that among its powerful needs is touching—human contact. Often making contact with another, The New Human Being—a combination of Homo Sapiens and Homo Biologicus—will add to the world's health and joys as the pioneer of a more loving, nurturing society."

Helen Colton
author of *The Gift of Touch* (G. P. Putnam's Sons)

"Hugging fosters a feeling of self-worth; it makes you more accepting of yourself...By helping you realize that you are a good person—a *huggable* person—it makes you want to take better care of that good person in order to keep that good person on the planet as long as possible."

Barbara Toohey & June Bierman
from *The Diabetic's Total Health Book*
(J. P. Tarcher)

Name: _____

Diagnosis: Touch deprivation

Treatment Plan: An abundance of hugs

Prognosis: Excellent

Other titles that will interest you...

My Mind Is Out to Get Me
Humor and Wisdom in Recovery
compiled by Dr. Ron B.

When recovering alcoholic Dr. Ron B. began attending Alcoholics Anonymous meetings, he was amazed by the rich oral tradition, wisdom, and humor found in sobriety. Unable to find a list of the slogans and sayings that changed his life, the author compiled these 500 inspirational quotes. Softcover, 168 pp. Order No. 1319

Today's Gift
Daily Meditations for Families

The tensions and joys that can help a family care for all its members are explored in these 366 meditations that nurture family esteem and strengthen family bonds. Softcover, 400 pp. Order No. 1031

For price and order information, or a free catalog, please call our Telephone Representatives.

HAZELDEN

1-800-328-9000 (Toll-Free, U.S., Canada and the Virgin Islands)	**1-651-213-4000** (Outside the U.S. and Canada)	**1-651-213-4590** (24 Hour FAX)

Pleasant Valley Road • P.O. Box 176 • Center City, MN 55012-0176
http://www.hazelden.org